Fallen Spirits

Volume 2

The Mind Monsters Series

By Diane Hatz

Fallen Spirits
©2024 by Diane Hatz

Fallen Spirits is Volume 2 in *The Mind Monsters Series* –
books2read.com/Fallen-Spirits

Volume 1, **Rock Gods & Messy Monsters**, is also available on Amazon and other retailers – books2read.com/RGMM

Visit dianehatz.com to sign up for the newsletter, read the blog, and more!

Cover design by Robin Vuchnich, My Custom Book Cover
1st edition, All rights reserved
Published by Whole Healthy Group LLC
Santa Fe, New Mexico
ISBN 979-8-9862823-6-7 (paperback)
ISBN 979-8-9862823-7-4 (e-book)
ISBN 979-8-9862823-8-1 (hardcover)
Library of Congress Control Number: 2024900241

No part of this publication may be reproduced, distributed, or transmitted in any form or by any means, including photocopying, recording, or other electronic or mechanical methods, without the prior written permission of the publisher, except as permitted by U.S. copyright law. For permission requests, please visit **dianehatz.com/contact-us/**

The story, all names, characters, and incidents portrayed in this production are fictitious. No identification with actual persons (living or deceased), places, buildings, and products is intended or should be inferred.

In order to rise from its own ashes,

a phoenix first must burn.

—*Octavia Butler*

Reviews

Toni Woodruff, *Independent Book Review*
"Wild, thrilling, weird, and beyond the scope of our reality (I think).

Fallen Spirits is an absolute whirlwind. Who in which world could connect such inter-dimensional insanity combined with the unbelievable truth of human reality like Diane Hatz has here.

...The worldbuilding is a mishmash of creativity; what Hatz dreams up, Hatz makes happen. Readers in love with the places language can take us will relish seeing what tricks the author has up her sleeve.

The ending leaves me wanting more from the installment...you'll get no other book like this one. Unless we count the first.

Imagination knows no bounds—or bowels—in this inventive, high-stakes sci-fi thriller."

Joslyn Vann, *US Review of Books*
"Hatz delivers a significantly more realistic and serious tale while continuing to provide a stinging critique of capitalism, corruption, abuse of power, and misogyny in the corporate world.

...Sensitive readers may be disturbed by scenes depicting sexual harassment and violence, but the author's intended message is clearly one of female empowerment, solidarity, healing, and redemption. Ending with a compelling cliffhanger, this book is the perfect setup for the next book in the series."

From the Author

Content Warning: This book contains potentially triggering subject matter, including profanity, alcohol consumption, sexual assault, abuse, and gross descriptions.

Dear Reader,

Fallen Spirits has a healthy peppering of expletives, graphic humor, and a few scenes that could possibly cause distress to some people.

The overall themes in *The Mind Monsters Series* are uplifting and inspirational, though the work also deals with issues some might find upsetting.

Fallen Spirits and *The Mind Monsters Series* in no way minimizes or excuses any type of unhealthy or abusive behavior; the intent is to do the opposite.

May you find your path and have the courage to follow it.

Enjoy!

Diane

Diane Hatz
Santa Fe, New Mexico

Chapter One

Alex's wildly improbable blonde hair was already streaked stress magenta and ill green. And it was only 9:00 a.m.

Sweat pooled in her armpits as she stared at her boss and ex-fiancé. The three months since their breakup were a blur of vodka and tears, but there was no more denying. Or wishful thinking. The creative conference she'd organized for his marketing firm Klein Strategies might have been a huge success, but that didn't matter. It had ended a few days earlier, so he had no use for her anymore. As much as Alex had avoided the truth, she knew this was it.

Finn's eyes were glued to his phone. Alex saw his leg bouncing up and down. She wanted to vomit. He'd kept her on these past months because she was his best experiential event designer, and she'd been too deep into planning the most exclusive wellness event his firm had ever organized to be successfully replaced. But he'd made her life a living hell by criticizing everything she did, arguing over every decision, or avoiding her altogether. Even her dreams had turned into nightmares about him.

Now was his chance to finish ruining her.

Finn looked briefly across the table, then back at his screen. "I have to let you go."

The last of Alex's broken heart fell to the ground. "What?" she spat, a mixture of hangover, bacon burrito, and stomach acid inching its way up her esophagus. The shock of finally hearing the words paralyzed her. She'd known this would happen, but false hope had been her only friend over the past few months as she struggled to make sense of what he'd done.

He glanced over her other shoulder. "You're fired."

Alex flinched again, still frozen to her seat. A piece of breakfast swirled in her mouth.

Finn glanced toward her. "I had no choice." His perfectly blue eyes and educated British accent cut into her soul and brought up more backwash bacon. "Corporate's reorganizing. You're terminated, effective immediately. Human resources will email your severance details."

Alex heaved as reality ripped her apart. He was corporate, the asshole. Her regurgitated breakfast burst from her mouth, covering Finn's desk and any last piece of denial she was trying to hide.

Finn jumped up. "What the fuck?"

Alex clamped her hand to her mouth, her eyes wide-open. She fought to keep more semi-digested egg, bacon, and tortilla from spilling out as it seeped through her fingers. Finn had just destroyed her plans, her dreams, her life.

She looked down, her shoulders slouched, her hand still firmly over her mouth. The ends of her magenta-and-green-streaked hair were splattered with vomit, as was her black Eileen Fisher ballet neck top.

There was nothing left. Alex heaved again. Everything was gone. At forty-five, how could she rebuild her life and find happiness?

Finn backed toward his office door. "Steve, get her out."

Her now ex-boss and former fiancé retched as he ran from the room. Abruptly, she deposited the last of her hope and breakfast on his desk, creating a pool of rejection and bad decisions.

"She's fucking insane," were the final words Finn uttered as he stormed down the hallway.

Security guard Steve stepped into the room, his forehead sprinkled with sweat. Gently, he took Alex's arm and helped her out of the chair.

Alex fumbled for a tissue as she stared at her parting gift to Finn. Red liquid swirled through the regurgitated mess, creeping across Finn's papers and antique wooden desk. The misery wine she'd downed the night before. Steve dry heaved as he led her out of her job and once-successful life.

Between her hangover and shock, everything was a blur. Her work colleagues scurried away like cockroaches. No one said goodbye, and no one would stay in touch. New York City friends could be so fleeting and conditional. In an instant, she'd been erased from a world she'd known for a decade. Another corporate throwaway.

Somehow, Alex gathered her belongings and was escorted to the midtown-Manhattan lobby. Security Steve left her and her Duane Reade bags at the front doors of the corporate monolith of her now-former life. Alex shivered as she stepped into the frigid February air, her coat half on and scarf askew. So many years wasted in that office building, all for nothing.

After losing her first love a decade ago out West, Alex had returned to New York, to the familiarity and few friends she had left. She'd needed time to heal and figure out her next steps before moving on. What she hadn't planned was meeting Finn and falling in love.

A tear welled up in Alex's eye. Frozen hearts and replaceable people plagued New York; returning had been a mistake.

She looked across the street and flinched. The bitter irony. Acht Records, her first career job, had been in that building. The corporate monolith had been a pleasant reminder of what she'd gotten away from. The blood-vessel explosions, the screaming, the insanity the entertainment industry was known for.

But here she was, twenty years later, the same failure.

She leaned against the cold marble of the skyscraper and buttoned her coat. Her magenta, green, black, and blue-streaked hair flew wildly about her in a rainbow of rage and despair. She picked up her bags as an Uber pulled to the curb.

As Alex started for the car, she glanced back at the building. She gasped as Finn walked through the revolving doors. Her bags fell—her spare shoes, makeup, and hand lotion spilling onto the sidewalk.

She hated herself for loving his perfectly handsome British and New York City kind of look. His early-forties peppered hair, perfect tan, and private-trainer, six-pack body dressed in a designer casual and tightly fitting coat were something most men were afraid to even dream of. She should have known he was too good-looking for her.

On Finn's heels was her now-former colleague and ex-friend, Maddie. Alex hadn't seen her in the three months since the split with Finn. Maddie nearly skipped out the door as Finn put his arm around her petite, twenty-something shoulders.

When Maddie turned, Alex felt a fist ram into her stomach, knocking the wind out of her. The baby bump was obvious, even through her formfitting puffer coat.

Although Alex was aware they were having an affair, seeing them together was too real. Knowing they were having a child cut her in half. Her knees buckled. She stumbled backward, her mascara rolling toward the curb.

Maddie caught Alex's eye. The ex-colleague smiled with triumphant glee as she held up her perfectly manicured, ungloved left hand and gave Alex a fourth-finger fuck you. A large diamond glistened in the sun.

Alex gasped again and stumbled back, her hand over her mouth. Her piece-of-shit former friend had stolen her lifelong dream.

***

"Evelyn, it's over."

Super-billionaire Jackson Thomas Wilson, known worldwide as JT, shifted uncomfortably in his chair. The founder of the online shipping and retail giant ShopMe noisily sipped his processed protein shake through a metal straw. His chief of staff usually broke up with his girlfriends, but Sal, his latest therapist, demanded he do it himself.

JT had agreed to end it by phone. Sal refused texting, and JT refused in person. This was their compromise.

"I don't dismiss staff," JT had said. "I pay people to do that."

"Maybe that's part of your problem," was the reply.

A voice brought JT back into the room. "Over? What's over?" came through his speakerphone in an unnatural, high-pitched tone.

"Pfffffftttt. Fffff." JT knew a bad decision when he made one, and this had been an awful choice. He readjusted himself and squeezed his butt cheeks. "Pfffffffffffft."

He looked at his notes, the ones his therapist had written and therefore approved. The billionaire was told to be nice, to use words Evelyn liked. He tried again and read from his script.

"I appreciate you, sweetie, and we've had some fun, but it's time to go our separate ways." JT rolled his eyes and emitted a quick "ffrrrttttt" at his own words.

"Separate ways?" screeched through the speaker. "Baby, what are you talking about? We're terrific together."

The global kingpin squeezed his ass even tighter, but "phhffrrrt-tt-phhreeeeeee-pffftt" still escaped. He was a self-made billionaire. He was in charge. He had claimed the idea for an app his colleague had mentioned at a dinner party one night.

Being a white male in Silicon Valley with an illogical idea, he immediately got funding. He took the millions and created a retail giant. That success led to more investors and more money to build a global consumer goods and shipping empire. JT became a multi-billionaire, so much so he was considered one of the richest men in the world. He was planning on becoming the first trillionaire. Why was he putting himself through an almost-in-person breakup?

At his six-month personal check-in with his accountant, JT learned he'd spent nearly half a million on Evelyn, including gifts, trips, and dates. A few days earlier, she'd asked for a monthly allowance. If he'd been getting what he wanted, he wouldn't have cared about the money. But Evelyn's refusal to play his bedroom games, or even have much sex with him, wasn't worth his investment.

"No, Evelyn, we're not terrific together. Let's keep this civilized." Sal had warned him she would protest.

"I am civilized," she screeched back. "What are you saying?"

No one ever spoke back or argued with JT. His face flushed. The familiar, unpleasant gurgling built again in his abdomen. He'd always had bad luck with women; even his wife, Celeste, was in the middle of divorcing him. For all his money and worldwide success, he couldn't find what he needed. Women only wanted what he had. He took another quick sip of his shake.

"This isn't a negotiation. We're done. I'm sending you a hundred thousand as a thank-you. But you have to sign something first." JT couldn't keep his butt squeezed much longer.

Evelyn's voice switched from high-pitched to pleading. "Baby, let me come over so we can talk about it. I'll do anything you want."

JT hated weakness, and she was crumbling like a house of cards. He pulled open his desk drawer and grabbed his new stress ball. Another suggestion from his shrink. Furiously, he squeezed and released as a quiet "pfffft" escaped each time his hand relaxed.

"No. We're over. What don't you understand? My lawyer will be in touch."

JT sensed Evelyn's panic turn to ice as it snaked through the phone.

"Don't you dare, you inconsiderate prick. How about I tell everyone you fart from your ass and your mouth?"

As anger boiled in his gut, JT held his butt together with superhuman force. His stomach danced a warning dance. "If you dare say anything about me, I'll sue. You signed the dating agreement our first night out. And I'll make sure you're never invited to an event. *Ever. Anywhere.* You'll spend the rest of your miserable life alone. With nothing."

"You mother...." were Evelyn's parting words as JT pounded his speakerphone off.

He threw the stress ball across his massive office as an explosive "squeeeeeee frrrrrrrt" escaped. It was a wet one. His goddamn doctors and medical researchers had better find a solution to his venting issue or he'd fire them all. Or worse. Ten years of research and all his scientists accidentally stumbled on was a procedure to extract energy from another dimension. And even though the invention would make him billions more, halting his anal expulsions was their top priority.

"Bret Horowitz is here," came through JT's intercom.

JT leaned back in his chair and groaned. This was all he needed. He sat in his shart and squirmed uncomfortably in the gooey ooze. Even the insulated, ultra-absorbent underpants his product development team had designed for him didn't always protect him.

"Make him wait. Get Five in here. I vented."

JT ignored the groan that slipped through his intercom. His fifth-ranked and lowest-level assistant, Five of Five, nervously entered the office with an assortment of towels and a black bag. JT kept five assistants on hand, all males and all replaceable parts he never wanted to know.

"It's close to a ten," JT said.

Five of Five rushed to JT's closet and pulled out spare underwear and JT's signature almost-jeans—black pull-on cotton with a touch of spandex pants with a mock fly. JT's venting was ranked from one to ten, with ten being an all-out fecal explosion. The lowest-ranked assistant was charged with cleaning up all the messes and had to sign multiple nondisclosure agreements before starting the job. Very few made it up the support-staff ladder past number five. Most quit after—or during—their first cleanup.

All were in fear of losing their careers—or lives—if they ever spoke about what they'd witnessed while working for JT. Several number Fives had disappeared, never to be seen again. They might have gone into hiding or been killed; the uncertainty was enough to keep the staff silent.

In a flash, Five of Five dashed back to his bag and snapped on rubber gloves. He grabbed a tarp from his supplies and placed it on the floor in front of his boss. The assistant lifted JT from his chair and leaned him against the desk on top of the plastic. He then pulled an extra-large adult body wipe from the bag. In one swift move, Five removed JT's pants and underwear and cleaned his boss's ass.

JT kept his eyes closed during Five's procedure. The explosions were bad enough, but other people knowing was too much. Especially when it was a wet one. He pretended it wasn't happening. If his eyes were closed, he could deny everything. JT was the gas in gaslighting.

In less than the regulation five minutes, Five of Five changed, cleaned, and redressed JT. The assistant gagged as he rolled up the tarp and shoved the soiled mess into a large, extra-reinforced, industrial-strength trash bag and raced out of the room. JT was confident he'd never see him again.

JT punched his intercom. "Keep holding Horowitz."

"Yes, sir," floated through the phone.

JT grabbed a key and spun around in his chair. He unlocked the drawer behind him, the one most people believed held his wild-game hunting rifle. But what he had was better.

The global kingpin reached in and reverently pulled out his black Darth Vader mask and lightsaber. He donned the helmet and stood. He turned on the voice and breathing controls and grabbed his sword. "Psssh-hew" filled his ears as the lightsaber glowed.

"Nnnnnnnnn" idled the sword as JT got into his death stance. He lifted the saber and cut through the air in his office, fighting unseen demons. A satisfying "wooomb, wooomb, wooomb" filled his ears.

JT sliced through imagined enemies until his breathing was as heavy as the sounds coming from his helmet. He walked into his executive bathroom and looked at himself. He stood as tall as his five-foot-five body would allow and threw back his shoulders, the lightsaber humming at his side.

"Jackson, I am your father," growled from behind the mask.

JT stared at his alter ego. He was invincible. The heavy breathing sounds of Vader filled the room. After several minutes of posing, he took a deep breath. He didn't want to, but it was time to return.

"Shwiii-ISHT" filled the air as the billionaire shut down his light sword. He turned off his helmet and removed it. He glanced in the mirror and looked away quickly. The balding, pudgy, middle-aged man with sad eyes who stared back wasn't him.

JT sighed and walked to his desk. With every stride, he stepped back into the cutthroat, power-hungry asshole he'd turned into.

Equipment safely locked away, he hit his intercom button. "Send him in."

The black steel doors opened. A briefcase bounced midair into the room. The front was emblazoned with the initials "BH." As it neared JT's desk, the case turned to its left. JT's personal lawyer, Bret Horowitz, appeared in front of him.

"Just admiring the view," the two-dimensional lawyer said as he faced JT. His nose and ears sprouted healthy amounts of wiry gray hair while his balding head sported a comb-over of thin, greasy bottle-black strands. He reached into his pocket and pulled out his box of smiles, putting on his wow-look-at-all-you-got semi-smile.

Emotion back in its box, Horowitz sat down, the tight-lipped line that was his mouth back in place. He set his briefcase on JT's desk and clicked it open.

Fresh and clean in his new clothing, JT leaned forward. The memory of what happened had left with his soiled clothes. "What now?"

"It's done."

Groaning, JT sat back and covered his eyes with his hand. "How much did I lose?" He must have paid off eight to ten women over the past five years. And now his wife, Celeste. What was wrong with them all?

Horowitz shifted in his seat, his haphazard comb-over sliding down his scalp and onto his forehead. "Nearly half."

Blood rushed to JT's face as he stared into his lawyer's emotionless eyes. "Half of everything?"

Horowitz nodded. "Half of everything we didn't hide." He ran his hand across his brow, pushing the fallen strands back onto his sweaty scalp. "Celeste has one of the best divorce lawyers in the country, and they went for everything."

JT was too angry to fart. "Do something. My lazy-ass ex-wife doesn't deserve half of everything I earned. It's my fucking money."

"She's not your ex yet, JT. And it's not worth it. Your legal bills on top of the settlement would be more than half."

JT pounded on his glass desktop, a surprise mini squirt splaying out his ass. Even though he had initially resisted wearing his definitely-*not*-adult-diaper underpants, with them he could ignore any micro-expulsions.

"We had a prenup."

Horowitz quickly tossed on his sympathy smile. As soon as it landed on his face, it was off and back in his box. "You filed for divorce before the ten-year mark, so you'll only pay alimony for five years. At least you have that." He shrugged. "Celeste claimed she didn't have time to go through the prenup and that you forced her to sign it."

JT snorted but kept silent.

"You're aware prenups don't always work," Horowitz said. "I have the best divorce experts on staff. And they concluded your agreement won't hold up in court." The lawyer didn't bother removing an emotion from his box. "And dating all those women over the past few years doesn't help. Like that girlfriend, Evelyn, you have now."

"She's gone. Another asshole trying to steal my money. Send her the breakup papers. She'll sign."

Horowitz stuck on and pulled off a satisfied smirk. "At least that's over. And she didn't cost much."

The lawyer rustled through his briefcase. "You can fight the divorce, JT, but let it go. Just pay. It'll cost you more to fight than settle." He looked at his client. "I'm telling you this even though I'd make a fortune off you."

"Pffftt." JT pulled open his top drawer and grabbed his Stormtrooper PEZ dispenser. "You've already made a fortune off me," he grumbled. He flipped open the helmet and shook a couple antacid pellets into his mouth. He quickly chewed and swallowed, then looked back at his lawyer.

"That bitch. She only married me for my money. How fucking stupid was I?"

"It happens. Don't beat yourself up." Horowitz pulled a thick stack of papers from his briefcase and placed them in front of JT. "You put everything you could in those overseas accounts. No one knows about them. That's a couple hundred million. We kept your Swiss accounts hidden. You're still an extremely wealthy man. Even with the divorce, you're a multi-billionaire and one of the richest people on the planet."

JT glared at his lawyer. "That's not fucking good enough. Celeste shouldn't be a billionaire because I'm one." He picked up the papers. "What's all this?"

"The settlement. I can take you through it."

JT dropped the pages onto his desk. "No. Just get the fuck out."

Horowitz stood, his box of smiles locked away. He pointed toward the six-inch high pile of papers. "Sign where all those Post-its are. Have your assistant make a copy for your records and messenger the original back to me."

JT let out an angry "ffffffffppppppppttt" and stared at the pages, ignoring him. He waited until Horowitz and his briefcase left the room.

He lifted his arms to throw the papers across the office but stopped. It would probably cause another ass explosion anyway. JT sat back in his chair. It was over. He knew a lost cause when he saw one. Nearly ten years living a lie.

When they'd met, JT was convinced it was love at first sight. He was sure Celeste was the one. His two close friends, his only two friends, had tried to warn him she was after his money, but he didn't believe them. Rather than face the truth, he'd kicked them out of his life and isolated himself. He brushed off the separate bedrooms, believing Celeste's excuse that she needed beauty time and space for her clothes. And with their own suites, it was easier to hide his bodily distress from her.

JT's innards gurgled as he signed page after page of the divorce settlement. Even though it had bored him, he'd tried the traditional way. He'd tried to make the marriage work and give her what she wanted. No more. Now he would conquer. Business *and* women.

When he finished signing, he punched his speakerphone. "One. Get this out of here. And get my acquisitions team. I want to buy something." JT looked out his window at the surrounding skyscrapers. "Like the biggest casino in Las Vegas. I want to own the biggest fuck-you monstrosity there is."

He turned toward his speakerphone. "And fire that useless shrink. Immediately."

Chapter Two

If the booze didn't kill her, the hangover might.

"Nooooooooo," Alex groaned as she turned over, her back aching from the soft sofa cushions she refused to replace. Her severance might last a year, but she wasn't buying anything until money started coming in. Her parents had taught her that.

She breathed deeply as her heart pounded furiously in her chest. She had passed out on the couch. Again.

She looked at the mess she'd become. Red wine had left a splattered design all over her shirt. Shards of glass littered the floor. She must have taken her drunken rage out on her wineglass and some framed photos of Finn. She couldn't remember.

Alex swung her legs to the floor, carefully navigating the clutter. She glanced around her Jersey City apartment, the one-bedroom she'd rented several months earlier when Finn had broken up with her and kicked her out of their downtown Manhattan condo. Her original plan was to live in Jersey temporarily until she bought her own place in Manhattan, but now that she was also jobless, this would be home for the foreseeable future.

A month's worth of post-employment wine and vodka bottles were scattered across the floor. Greasy food delivery containers from the past two weeks covered her kitchen counter, coffee table, and the TV trays she'd placed around the room—furniture she'd found on the side of the street. Repurposing roadside trash was the mark of a true New Yorker.

Alex gagged as she breathed in souring alcohol and rotting food, her hair a mixture of ill green, stress magenta, and hopeless blue. It reminded her of the last day she'd seen Finn. She heaved again. She already had a doozy of a headache.

She slid her hands beneath her and pushed herself off the couch, her brain thick with hangover haze. She refused to step on the scale, but her aching joints and general heaviness were warning her she was putting on too much weight. And yoga pants were deceiving.

She stumbled forward to go to the bathroom.

"Fuck!" Alex screamed to the walls as she jumped. A large piece of glass stuck out of the bottom of her foot. She yanked it free, ignoring the blood that dripped and mixed with the wine stains that had seeped into the floorboards.

"This has to stop," she yelled to the room. Alex steadied herself, willing the nausea away.

With a grunt, she limped around the mess to the kitchen, her hair streaking blacker by the second. Alex rummaged under the sink, grabbing several heavy-duty trash bags.

Splotches of blood left a trail behind her as she hobbled back to the living area. "He can fire me. He can fuck me over for someone younger." She grabbed the first bottle she came to and threw it into the bag. "And he can go fuck himself."

Alex forgot her foot as she stormed around the room, leaving more droplets of blood in her wake. She tossed bottles and food containers into the trash bag. When she got dizzy, she stopped and steadied herself. She ignored the tears that rolled down her cheeks.

"Fuck this. Fuck booze," she screamed, then looked at her bookshelf. "And fuck you, Finn."

Alex grabbed the photos she hadn't destroyed yet and stuffed them into the trash. She relished the sound of glass breaking as she stomped around, throwing away her leftover food, booze, and soured memories.

She dropped two full bags of leftover Finn next to the front door and sat down to catch her breath. Her nausea danced in her stomach as she stared at the trash. "You're where you belong, you piece of garbage."

She glanced around her dirty, though somewhat picked-up, apartment and sighed. "Now what?"

As she stared at the blank walls and nearly empty bookcase, she realized most of the pictures in her apartment had been of Finn or Finn and herself. Even though they'd broken up, she hadn't been able to say goodbye. *Enough*, she thought. *This has to stop.*

She left two framed photos of her beautiful labradoodle, Tara. Fuckhead Finn had even taken her.

Alex caught her breath as reality once again exploded inside her. No job, no husband, no kids, no real friends. Nothing. She swallowed her emptiness and the leftover pizza trying to get out. She was nothing. Why was she ever born?

She stumbled to the door and grabbed a trash bag. Quickly, she opened it, emptying her masticated pizza and acidic juices into the mess, aiming for any photos of Finn she saw.

"Enough of this shit. Enough feeling sorry for myself," she said emphatically to the empty room.

Alex found a somewhat-clean sweater and black leggings and threw them on. The shower would have to wait. She groaned as she bent over and put a Band-Aid on her cut. She found her coat and sneakers and slipped them on. Her joints ached from lack of exercise.

She grabbed her backpack and both bags of trash and left her apartment for the first time in over a week. Even though it was cloudy, she cringed and closed her eyes at the brightness. She dropped the trash and pulled out her sunglasses. After putting them on and slipping her pack over her shoulders, she picked up the last few reminders of her former life.

She threw the trash into the nearly full industrial container. Grabbing the cover, she hit the bags over and over, forcing the garbage in and her anger out. She slammed the lid onto the bin, shoving down the last bits of Finn.

Alex headed to her neighborhood health food store and picked up fruit and some nutritious-enough food. On her way home, she slowed as she passed Jersey Wines.

To diversify her booze buying, she regularly rotated liquor stores in the area. Alex told herself it was for variety, but underneath her lie she knew the amount of alcohol she was drinking embarrassed her. She didn't want the store clerks judging her.

Alex stopped. She hadn't bought anything from there for at least two weeks. She could limit her drinking and control it. A glass or two never hurt. And keeping a couple bottles at home for guests was a good idea.

Her feet were inside the store before she realized what she was doing. Automatically, Alex grabbed two half-gallon bottles of vodka and four bottles of wine. At the register, she added two packs of cigarettes for good measure. After staggering out under the weight of her purchases, she slowly made her way home.

At the corner she stopped, out of breath. The bags were too heavy, so she put them down.

"Hi" floated toward Alex.

Alex turned to her right. A heroin-chic waif of a woman walked toward her, sporting a black leather biker jacket, white T-shirt, black skinny jeans, and black Converse sneakers. She was chewing gum loudly. Her straight black hair bobbed at her shoulders while her bangs swished back and forth. "Can you help me, please?"

Alex stiffened, her hair streaking black. "I don't have any money." She reached down and grabbed her bags. "And I'm not giving you anything."

"Money? Oh, I don't want money." The stranger cracked her gum.

Alex released her grip and placed her purchases back on the sidewalk. She looked at the young woman. Her voice was warm and soft—soothing, in fact. As she gazed into her piercing gray, exotic eyes, Alex softened. There was something familiar and friendly about the stranger. And she'd never seen eyes so...otherworldly. "What do you want then?"

The woman blew a bubble and continued in her quiet tone, a total contradiction to how she looked. "I'm lost."

Alex didn't trust strangers who talked to her on the street, especially in Jersey City. At seventeen, after moving from the blue-collar Philly suburb she'd grown up in, she'd lived in safe spaces with doormen and security systems. The part of Jersey City she now found herself in made her uncomfortable. "Where you going?"

The woman continued to crack her gum, a look of confusion coloring her face. She shrugged. "That's the problem. I don't know."

"I can't help." Alex reached for her bags again.

"Please. I'm not sure what to do."

Alex exhaled loudly and straightened. "Here." She handed the two heaviest bags to the young woman. "Help me get these home, and I'll see what I can do."

The young woman took the bags with delight. "Oh, thank you."

Both remained silent as they walked to Alex's apartment on the next block. Alex was renting what realtors called a historic brownstone. In reality, it was a small, one-bedroom apartment in a former three-story family row home away from the high rises on the water. The waterfront condos housed successful executives who worked in New York City, and Alex was no longer one of them.

When they reached the front door, the stranger said, "I'm sorry, but I have to go to the bathroom. Could I use yours?"

Alex tensed. "Not today."

The woman looked up and down the street. "There's nowhere I can go." She opened her biker jacket. "And I've got nothing to hide, see?"

Alex hesitated, her hand on her doorknob. "I don't think so."

The punk-looking person with the soothing voice put down the two bags and shook off her coat. She stood in her T-shirt in the chilly March air and handed her leather jacket to Alex. "Look. There's nothing on me. Frisk me."

Alex realized she hadn't spoken to anyone in over two weeks, so she grabbed the coat from the stranger and opened her door. "It's a bit of a mess," she said as they walked inside.

The stranger nodded and cracked her gum.

"It's to the left of the fridge."

The woman rushed to the bathroom and closed the door.

Alex brought the bags to her kitchen area and placed them on the counter before turning on the electric kettle.

When the stranger emerged from the bathroom, Alex said, "Do you have a name?"

She shrugged and shook her head. "No."

Alex looked out her one window to the concrete front garden. The large faux-crystal ball her landlord loved was sitting on its cracked concrete stand. It sparkled in the late-afternoon sun.

"How about we call you Crystal until we figure it out?"

The woman nodded and blew a bubble.

Alex pointed to a chair at the table. "Tea or coffee?"

"Tea, please," Crystal said as she took a seat and picked at her black nail polish. She looked up. "Could I have my jacket back?"

Alex picked up the jacket and squeezed the leather from top to bottom. There was nothing sharp or unusual in it. She handed it back to Crystal.

After Alex placed a cup of tea in front of Crystal and made a mug of coffee for herself, the two women sat across from each other in an awkward silence. Alex glanced at the bags on the counter. A hair of the dog would be perfect. She shook her head and turned back to Crystal. The drinking was over. At least until six.

"What do you remember?"

Crystal wadded her gum into a ball and stuck it on the side of her mug. "I've been in Jersey City for a little while, I think. My memory fades in and out, though, so I'm not sure how long. I became fully conscious a few hours ago. Not far from here."

Alex stared at the gum and looked down her nose in disgust. "Wait," she said. "You could be on vacation and hit your head." She leaned forward. "Or worse. Maybe you were kidnapped and escaped."

Crystal blew on her tea and took a sip. She lowered her cup. "It's weird. I'm sure I'm in New Jersey, and I know general things, but I don't remember any details about myself."

Alex looked at the stranger with the beautiful, otherworldly gray eyes sitting across from her. "You should go to a hospital. You probably hit your head. You could have amnesia or a concussion."

"Can you drive me?" Crystal asked in a warm yet direct tone. Her words seemed more a statement than a question.

Alex's hair streaked anger black. She'd helped others enough in her life. "No."

"Please."

"I'll get you an Uber." Alex grabbed her phone, then realized she hadn't charged it for at least a week. She dropped it on the table.

"Please take me."

Alex studied the stranger in her kitchen. She was so familiar, yet not. Hard yet soft. A contradiction on many levels. The bottle of vodka called to her again. *Just one drink.* She looked through her remaining hangover haze and sighed. If she got rid of Crystal, she could have all the drinks she wanted.

Alex stood. "If that's how I get you out of here, let's go."

***

The women hopped into Alex's BMW hybrid and headed toward the closest urgent care. As Alex turned down Montgomery Street, she noticed a black SUV close in on her bumper. It had come out of nowhere. She sped up and headed down the road. Damn carjackers.

The forceful jolt snapped their heads forward and back. Crystal's gum flew from her mouth. Alex's car lurched forward.

"What the...?" Alex looked in her rearview mirror, her hair anger black and shock white. The SUV had rammed the back of her car. Her knuckles were white as she gripped the wheel.

"This is my fucking car. The only nice thing I have left, you assholes." She glared into her rearview mirror as she pressed the accelerator. It made no sense that carjackers would ruin a car they were trying to steal.

As Alex weaved in and out of traffic, the SUV stayed right behind them. She maneuvered around cars, pedestrians, and cyclists.

"What should I do?" she asked as the SUV stayed on her tail. "If we stop, who knows what'll happen? My luck, they'll have guns."

She glanced at her passenger. Crystal's face and body were fading. She was becoming transparent. Alex blinked hard and shook her head; Crystal was back in focus. The hangovers were getting worse. She seriously needed to quit drinking.

Alex glanced in her rearview mirror: the SUV was barreling toward them.

"Hold on!" she yelled to Crystal.

Every muscle in Alex's body froze as she braced for impact. The forceful jolt threw them forward, their seatbelts snapping them back against their seats. The sound of metal crushing metal unleashed a fury buried in Alex's chest.

"Motherfuckers!"

Alex flattened her foot to the floor, her jaw tight and body stiff. Her now pure-black anger hair flew wildly about her. She looked in her mirror again as two men in black army fatigues jumped out of the SUV. They looked less like carjackers and more like secret military forces she'd seen in movies.

"Come on, you piece of shit."

Metal screeched against metal as the BMW slowly broke free from the two-car crushed tangle. Tire smoke and burning rubber filled Alex's nose.

The two men reached her car window. Alex slammed her hand hard on her horn as the BMW leapt forward. She kept the accelerator pressed down. Pedestrians crossing the street jumped back to the sidewalk, and cars pulled to the curb as she sped through.

She lightened up on the gas and glanced in her side mirror. The two men were jumping into their car. She looked at the road. The entrance to Route 9 was just ahead.

As Alex turned the BMW onto the highway, she checked the rearview mirror. The SUV swerved in front of an elderly lady slowly crossing the street with her overflowing shopping cart. The bumper grazed the cart, sending cans and groceries flying into the air.

Alex sped west. When she looked in her mirror again, the SUV was nowhere in sight. Sighing with relief, she glanced at Crystal. "I think we're okay. At least for now."

Crystal fumbled in her pocket and unwrapped a stick of gum.

"Make sure you find that gum you spit out."

"Sure." Crystal leaned forward and searched the floor of the car with her hand.

"This is so fucked up." Alex kept her foot on the accelerator but eased back to a solid seventy miles an hour. "My car's ruined."

Crystal leaned back, a lint-covered ball of used gum in her hand. "I'm sorry." She unzipped the top front pocket of her biker jacket and dropped it inside.

"Whatever," Alex said. "I'm not surprised, considering how my life's going." She let out a sarcastic laugh as she passed an eighteen-wheeler on the crowded road. "My ex bought it anyway. This thing should be demolished and join everything else he ruined for me."

Crystal looked out the back window at the crumpled mess of a trunk. "Guess it's time for something new." She turned back to Alex and smiled warmly. "Change is good."

Alex ignored her comment as they neared Newark. "I'll find a hospital or urgent care and drop you off."

"Would you mind staying on the road?"

Alex heard the soft urgency in Crystal's voice as strands of her hair turned blacker. "I can't cart you around the universe."

Crystal straightened in her seat and looked at her with her piercing gray eyes. "We're in danger."

Alex stiffened and pressed harder on the gas. "What? What kind of danger?"

Crystal shook her head, her shoulder-length black bob and bangs swaying. "No idea. I just know we are. You have to keep going."

Alex cursed her hangover brain. The woman could be delusional. She was definitely dramatic. Or she could be a pathological liar. Or... Alex hadn't thought of this. She could be the kidnapper.

Alex sighed. Or she could be telling the truth. One of them might be in danger. What if the SUV that rammed them wasn't full of carjackers? They could be after Crystal. Worse yet, would Finn have hired someone?

Fuzzy thoughts bounced around Alex's head. Life-changing decisions often came from a small yes or no, and she had a feeling this was a turning point.

She weaved through traffic. She could return to her lonely lack of an existence, or she could face a future full of the unknown. A safe today or an unpredictable tomorrow.

Alex hesitated as the exit quickly approached. She eased her foot off the gas. She blinked, took a deep breath, and pressed the accelerator back to the floor, sailing past the exits to Newark.

There was nothing to live for, so it didn't matter if she went west.

Again.

***

As they headed into West Virginia, Crystal spoke up. "Will we ever stop?"

Alex glanced over. "You okay?"

"My right leg's burning. And my whole body's sore."

"Probably the jolt from that SUV. Why don't we eat? We need gas anyway. We're running on fumes."

Crystal nodded and cracked her gum.

Alex glanced in her side mirror.

"If they were behind us, they would have found us by now," Crystal said.

Alex exited the freeway in Morgantown, West Virginia, and turned into the first gas station they saw. She got out and looked at the back of her car. The trunk was so mangled there wasn't one anymore. Her bumper was missing, and her crushed license plate dangled at a precarious angle. But it still held on. Like her. At least the frame wasn't rubbing against the tires.

"Ah, fuck it," she muttered as she turned away and put the nozzle into her tank. At least the car still ran, and no gas was leaking. While the car was filling, she hurried into the gas station mini-mart and pulled a few hundred dollars from the ATM. Better safe than sorry.

On her way to the car, Alex spotted a Cracker Barrel sign up the hill. She got back into the driver's seat and pointed out the window. "Not normally my first choice, but it'll have to do."

Crystal nodded.

They drove to the restaurant and found the last open spot in the back.

"Well, it's definitely popular," Crystal said.

Alex nodded as they walked through the parking lot jammed with cars.

After checking in with the hostess, they went into the Cracker Barrel country store. They wandered through the candy, snow globes, and assorted trinkets no one needed but many convinced themselves they had to have. Modern marketing at its best.

Crystal took her hands out of her motorcycle jacket and picked up a large brown ceramic owl teapot. "What do people do with all this stuff?"

Alex shrugged. "Beats me." She picked up an electric, glowing snow globe and peered at the silver figure inside. "Ah. A musical, lighted, angel glitter globe. Now that's something we all need." When she turned, Crystal gasped. Alex laughed. "Did this scare you?" She turned it over in her hand. "It is quite ugly."

"No," Crystal said. "But there's something about it."

Alex shrugged. It was a snow globe, a glass ball of glitter and water. With an angel glued in the middle. It was tacky but nothing to get excited over. "You okay?"

"Not sure," Crystal said. "There's something about that globe."

Alex glanced around. She noticed the shop clerk quickly avert her eyes. She'd been watching them.

"I don't feel well," Crystal said as she began to fade from sight.

Alex blinked several times to clear her vision, but she could see through Crystal like she was a ghost.

"What the...?"

Crystal put another stick of gum in her mouth. She chewed quickly as her hands trembled.

Just then, their reservation buzzer vibrated. Alex pulled it out of her pocket. When she glanced at Crystal again, she could see her clearly. Alex shook her head to brush off what she couldn't believe; it had to be her hangover.

"You're probably hungry," Alex said. "Our table's ready, and I'm starving."

"Can we get some gum?" Crystal asked. "I'm almost out." She shrugged. "It helps me."

Alex nodded. She avoided looking at the clerk as she bought half a dozen packs for Crystal.

They were soon seated and looking over the extensive menu.

"This place has everything," Crystal said.

Alex nodded as she flipped through the pages to the back. "Yeah, except alcohol. I need a drink."

"Not if you're driving," Crystal said.

Alex made a snide face but said nothing. She glanced up and noticed the store clerk staring at them from the entranceway by the hostess podium. The cashier quickly averted her eyes when she saw Alex look.

Alex leaned toward Crystal. "That store employee is staring at you. She was also eyeing us in the store. Do you think she's with those men from Jersey?"

Crystal looked toward the hostess area, but the employee was gone. She turned back to Alex and shrugged. "That might be stretching it a bit. How would they figure out we were here? I'm sure it's nothing."

"A strange black SUV tried to run us off the road," Alex said. "I think everything right now is something."

They ordered and were soon eating the largest all-day breakfasts they'd ever seen. When they finished, Alex took the leftover biscuits, wrapped them in a paper napkin, and nonchalantly stuffed them into her backpack.

"What are you doing?" Crystal started.

Alex tossed in a handful of strawberry, grape, and mixed jelly packets. "Food for later."

After she paid the bill and headed to the exit, she noticed the clerk standing at the doorway.

"Come back soon," the woman said as they walked by.

Alex nodded. They stepped outside into darkness and pouring rain.

"Shit," escaped Alex's mouth as they both ran to the back of the lot. She shivered as cold water seeped through her clothes.

They jumped into the car. Alex started the engine and cranked up the heat, her whole body shaking. As she pulled the BMW out of her spot, Crystal pointed out the front window. Alex followed her finger. The store clerk waved frantically as she ran toward them in the downpour.

"Look," Crystal said. "She's motioning for you to roll down your window. She looks upset."

Against her better judgment, Alex opened her window. Rain splattered in.

The clerk hastily handed a plastic bag to her. "There's no time. They're here."

"What...?"

"I'm telling you, there's no time," the woman said, a frantic tone coloring her words. "Those men in that black SUV chasing you? They're here."

Terror ripped through Alex. "How do you...?"

"No time. My friend's distracting them, but you only have a minute or two. There's food and an address in the bag. Go there as fast as you can. They'll explain."

Alex froze, her mouth open in shock. The clerk grabbed her shoulder. "I'm one of the good guys. I'm trying to help. Get the hell out of here. *Now.*" She turned away, then looked back. "Throw away your cell phones. They're tracking you."

Shocked, Alex stared at the woman. "How do you...how do you...?" she stammered.

"*Go!*" yelled the clerk.

Alex closed her window and went into autopilot. She put the car in drive and screeched out of the space, heading back toward the interstate. As she squinted to see through the pouring rain, her stomach turned over its newly eaten contents.

She turned to Crystal. "Open the bag and get the address."

Crystal reached in and pulled out a slip of paper. "Wait. Your phone. She said to throw away your phone."

"No," Alex said, concentrating on the road. "It's still new." She pressed the accelerator and merged onto the freeway.

Crystal picked up Alex's backpack and pulled out her phone.

"No!" Alex screamed, trying to reach for her bag.

Crystal opened the window and tossed the phone onto the rain-soaked highway, then turned to Alex. "It doesn't matter how new your phone is if you're dead."

Alex caught her breath. The windshield wipers swept back and forth as rain beat against the roof of the car. Bright headlights appeared as dots in her rearview mirror, swerving from side to side. She pressed the gas pedal hard as the car climbed up the mountainous road.

"Wait," Crystal said, reading the slip of paper. "It says to take exit sixty-eight." She pointed at the green road sign quickly coming toward them. "There. It's the next one."

Enormous pools of water sprayed up around them as Alex moved to the right lane and sped off the freeway. Glancing over, she saw the confused look on Crystal's face. "What!" she screamed over the noise of the rain as her fingers clung to the steering wheel.

"It says pull into the truck stop and drive to the gas pumps."

Alex steered the car to the covered fueling area. "Let's hope we're at the right place."

A stern-looking man jumped out from the pumps. His small round glasses, receding hairline, and farmer overalls made him look eerily like the male in Grant Wood's *American Gothic*. All he needed was a pitchfork. He motioned for them to pull up behind a silver Ford Fusion.

As Alex pulled next to him, he grabbed the door handle and yanked it. "Get out," he barked through the closed window.

Alex put the car in park and jumped out. The rain pounded against the metal roof above them. A similarly grim-looking woman stood by the sedan in front of them, her wrinkles knitted harshly around her mouth and her hair pulled back in a tight bun. The doors were open, the engine running.

Frantically, she motioned for them to come over. "Get in!" she exclaimed as Alex and Crystal approached the car.

"I don't—" Alex started.

"No time." The woman grabbed Alex's arm and pushed her into the car, while the man gently placed Crystal in the passenger seat. "Get in and drive. There's a map in the glove box with the address and route highlighted. Don't speed. Act like any tourist. But get the hell out of here."

The man handed the restaurant bag to Crystal and closed her door.

The couple jumped into Alex's crumpled car as headlights pierced through the rain and raced toward them. Casually, Alex drove away, like any car after gassing up. Her heart pounding in her ears, she pulled back onto the interstate.

Alex's former BMW raced by on her left, as if to get away. She looked at her crumpled car as it passed them, then peered into the passenger window and caught the man's eye. He nodded curtly, with a grave expression.

"Shit," Alex exclaimed. "My backpack. I left it in the car."

"Does it have all your money and everything?"

"No," Alex said as she pounded on the steering wheel. "My money, credit cards, and license are on me. But my sunglasses, makeup, all my stuff." She glanced at Crystal. "It was mine. I've got nothing now."

Alex and Crystal turned away as a black SUV sped by, doing at least a hundred miles an hour. As Alex slowed to the speed limit, her stomach somersaulted with anxiety.

"Well, at least you have your life." Crystal chomped her gum and ran her hand across the black leather console. "And this is a nice car."

Alex stared straight ahead, her fingers glued to the steering wheel. "Now's not the time to discuss the automobile's beauty."

"Well, at least it solved the problem with your BMW." Crystal leaned back and cracked her gum.

Alex glanced to her right as they passed her beamer and the SUV on the shoulder. Four men in black military fatigues surrounded her old car. She looked at the woman in the driver's seat and sensed the stranger's relief as she and Crystal escaped. Alex drove by, leaving the last bit of Finn and her former life behind.

***

"OA on line one," floated through JT's intercom.

JT hit the button next to the blinking light; Operation Angel was his top priority. "Did you get her?"

"Sir, they got away."

His stomach erupted. "What?!" He grabbed his stormtrooper dispenser from his top drawer and tossed three super-strength prescription antacids into his mouth. He downed them with his usual overly-processed protein shake.

The deep-throated, military-style voice continued. "They evaded us."

"Ffrrrrrrrrt." JT squeezed his cheeks and tossed a few more antacids into his mouth. "What's wrong with you morons?" he said, chewing loudly. "How could they escape? You're supposed to be an elite military force."

The voice didn't waver. "Sir, we caused a civilian injury. We had to stop."

JT's fists clenched tighter and tighter as he willed his ass to stay dry. "What kind of injury?"

"An elderly woman, sir. She's fine, but we clipped her. We destroyed her shopping cart."

JT snapped his stormtrooper head open and closed. "Who cares about an old lady and her Metamucil? You should have kept going."

"Can't do that, sir. No civilian casualties. We weren't sure how bad she was, so we had to stop." There was a slight pause. "We rammed the car we were chasing, so it's damaged. And we got the license plate. It should be easy to find."

"Something at least," said JT.

The billionaire jotted down the license number and slammed his fist on the intercom button, cutting off the call and cracking his phone. The goons had lost her. Quickly, he unlocked his cabinet, grabbed his lightsaber, and turned it on. "Wooomb, wooomb, wooomb" filled his ears as he sliced into his anger.

A loud but dry "Pssssshhhhhffrrppth" filled the air. JT flinched at his own smell. He slashed through invisible demons as he battled his way back to his phone.

"One. Fire the OA team. Hire another group. And get me info on the owner of this car."

JT gave the plate number and slammed off his intercom, cracking the phone even more. One of his five assistants had better notice the phone needed replacing and get new equipment there in the next hour. Or he'd fire them all. JT safely locked his lightsaber away and sat back at his desk.

The intercom buzzed again.

"What!" he screamed into the plastic machine.

"Your Society meeting is in an hour. Should I get the car?"

JT's body rumbled louder, but thankfully he remained fecal-free. The new antacids his scientists had created just might be working. "What do you think, you idiot? Figure it out."

JT cut off his assistant and hit the human resources button.

"Yes, JT," came wearily over the phone.

"Fire One. Two is now One. Bump the rest up. Get someone for Five."

"Yes, JT."

JT clicked off. He leaned back in his chair, his stomach growling to its own tune. Firing a few people usually cheered him up, and he'd hopefully destroyed at least five lives that morning—the four military goons and his assistant. But JT wasn't satisfied like he normally was. He needed to up his domination game.

An hour later, he circled 72nd Street, quiet but dry "poot poot poots" filling his custom-built, luxury Aston Martin, a nod to his favorite band, The Beatles. JT recently discovered Paul McCartney's actual 1964 car was going up for auction; it was already his.

Thirty minutes after the meeting started, his driver arrived at the Upper East Side mansion. JT tossed a few stormtrooper tabs into his mouth and got out.

Before he could ring the bell, the door silently opened. JT stepped into the grand foyer of The Society for Advanced Economics, or The Society, as he and his fellow members called the club. It was a super-secret organization a group of globally powerful, über-wealthy European and American men had formed in the 1970s.

The original gathering had started as a joke and a not-so-friendly race to become the world's first trillionaire. All but one of the original ten white men were dead, with a new generation of power brokers and global controllers taking their place. The cabal had even expanded in celebration of diversity—two Asians and one Jewish tycoon were now included. Women and blacks...well, The Society could only go so far.

JT was confident he'd be the first to make the trillionaire mark, even with his divorce. His latest technology, which could reach into other dimensions of space-time, might not stop his venting issue, but it would make him billions more than his globally successful, astonishingly profitable ShopMe empire.

The online retail and shipping giant made his way to the conference room. When he walked in, he noticed six empty chairs. Meetings would soon be over before they started because the other mega-rich elite of The Society spent most of their time trying to arrive later than others in a childish display of power and strength. What assholes.

JT nodded offhandedly at the four titans around him. He stayed butt dry as he took his unofficially official seat. For meetings with peers, he minimized any eruptions by wearing his extra-super-protective underwear and sealing up his bottom with absorbent butt plugs. "Ass tampons," an ex once remarked. JT literally threw her out his front door the instant the words came out of her mouth.

An attendant who served but was not seen placed a coffee in front of him. Workers at The Society not only signed confidentiality agreements but also handed over control of their lives when they started employment. If they leaked any information, The Society terminated them. Not fired them, but killed them on the spot.

Employees also had to agree to the invisibility procedure, one of JT's early side inventions and another byproduct of his doctors' and scientists' attempts to quell his venting issues. Once hired, staff had cloaking chips implanted in their necks so they were invisible to Society members. Ignoring service workers was easy enough, but not having to look at them made visiting Society headquarters much more enjoyable.

Even with rumors of employee assassinations and inhumane treatment of staff, hundreds of applicants slipped résumés through the front door every month, reinforcing JT's belief that he and his colleagues were a more advanced species. He never considered that desperate people might endure injustices in order to survive.

"JT," came in a slow Texan drawl from across the table.

JT looked up and saw a white-haired, well-tanned, chiseled-face man sporting a ten-gallon hat. The plastic surgery concealed his age and had removed any natural features.

"Sam McMahon," JT said, acknowledging the world's biggest oil, gas, and aerospace tycoon. "How's it going?"

McMahon gave JT a small shrug and tipped his cowboy hat back. "Seems I'm lower than a rattlesnake in a wagon rut." He shoved an unlit cigar in his mouth and chewed on it.

JT faked an ounce of concern. "Oil prices again?"

McMahon nodded and removed his Texas pacifier. "Yes, sir." He leaned forward, an oil-slick sneer sliding across his face. "You've been up to no good."

JT put on his best modestly immodest smile. "I don't know what you're talking about."

All eyes turned toward the commotion at the doorway as the five remaining members made way for the other to go through first. They all settled into their unofficially official seats, their preferred coffee automatically appearing in front of them. Watson, the British aristocrat with dubious ties to European royalty, looked especially proud of himself for being the last to saunter in.

As the current Society president, McMahon brought his gavel down on the antique mahogany table. "I call this meeting to order."

"I second," military and defense magnate Richard Moulder said, fulfilling his role as vice president.

McMahon fumbled in his crocodile leather briefcase and brought out several sheets of paper. "Notes from the last meeting are in your private email accounts. Any updates?"

A large, round, red-faced man with an impressive beer belly spoke up. "I have update."

"Go, Orlov," McMahon replied.

"Seems Russian president is in little argument with Chinese premier. Nuclear war maybe finally going to happen."

A short Asian man stood up. "I hear same. We must talk after, Orlov, and figure out what we can do. No nuclear war. Got enough problem with that crazy North Korean."

Oligarch Dmitri Orlov grunted a nod. "Right after, Wang."

Real estate tycoon Chen Wang nodded.

"Anything else?" asked McMahon.

Luxury goods and fashion guru Paul Whitley sat back in his chair and pointed across the table. "I found out JT's screwing with space-time." He glared at JT. "What the fuck you doing?"

McMahon pulled out his electromagnetic server checker and clicked it, making double sure no unseen staff were in the room. The Society president leaned forward as all eyes turned to JT.

Moulder piped up. "Yeah, JT, what are you doing? Bylaws say you have to share anything new."

JT fumed. Although he couldn't keep his latest project a secret any longer, he did have a couple years' head start. "I can't share much. You know, top-level trade-secret stuff. And it's still being developed. But…" He paused and sat back for effect, then leaned forward again. "I can reach into other dimensions."

Murmurs of disbelief buzzed around the table.

JT smiled his corporate fake smile, a combination of disdain and manufactured nonchalance. "In short," he continued, "I'm exploring alternate space. Other dimensions." He studied his competition. "Some of you have exclusive deals with aliens like the Yakadans, so I figured the Milky Way was under contract with at least one of you. Therefore, I've gone in another direction."

A chuckle of shared arrogance filled the room.

The young, squeaky tech savant with pasty white skin raised his hand. McMahon shook his head. "You don't raise your hand, Minor."

"Oh, yeah, right." Aaron Minor bounced in his chair, his limbs banners of anxiety. At forty-five, he was The Society's youngest member—and the top technology and social media genius in the world. And wealthiest. Minor turned his anxious eyes in the retail giant's direction. "We're aware of that, JT. But there's more. Just come out with it."

"Agreed," McMahon replied. "Stop bullshitting."

JT looked at the table; he couldn't avoid it this time. He wanted to keep this discovery to himself, but he had no choice. "Seems my scientists discovered how to extract energy from spirits."

A murmur of surprise filled the room.

"What do you mean?" Minor asked, his voice higher pitched than usual, his arms nervously flailing about like a car dealership plastic-tube air dancer.

"I mean," JT said, "those stories about angels and spirits and all that. They're true. Other dimensions exist in the universe. Not just aliens on other planets. Spirits exist that help guide humans."

Abruptly, McMahon sat back in his chair, his hat falling to the floor. "Well, I'll be a shotgun son of a buck."

Aaron Minor sat on his hands. "I don't believe you."

The pharmaceutical giant sitting across from JT spoke up. "You're messing with the divine nature of the universe. This could cause trouble you can't imagine."

JT snorted. "You and your spirituality, Chowdhury. I'm not messing around with God. Just a few spirits." He looked around the room again, absorbing the collective stupidity. "Did any of you read the global consumer trends report from last month? Consumers are buying less. They're simplifying, downsizing. They're beginning to shun materialism."

"So?" Chowdhury asked.

"Seriously?" JT glanced around the room, genuinely surprised. "None of you get it, do you?"

"Enlighten us," McMahon drawled, his hat back in place.

JT took a deep breath to loosen the growing ball of aggravation in his stomach. "When people simplify, they buy less. They're too busy dancing with wolves in Wyoming or singing 'The Sound of Music' on a mountain." He paused and glared at everyone at the table. "And they won't buy our stuff."

"I've heard a growing number of people are quitting their jobs for no reason these days," Moulder chimed in.

"If we don't do something, people will stop buying stuff they don't need," said JT. "Our profits will plummet." He paused for effect. "And we won't have enough people working for us, making us money."

Men had invented materialism to control others and make an elite few rich and powerful. These select few, like those around the table, could lose their elevated standing if the average person cured their addiction to consumerism. JT refused to accept that possibility.

"Damn, that's some cheese fallin' off my crackers," McMahon said. He stuck his cigar back in his mouth and gave it a good suck.

"Well, what are you doing?" Moulder asked.

JT paused; he hated giving away ideas for inventions. And handing over business plans to other billionaires was infuriating. His stomach pounded in protest. He tried to keep his mouth shut and breathe through his nose, but the force was overpowering.

The agreement to join The Society was legally binding. They all had to share ideas about new projects. This helped with developing complementary products and services they could each make money from. They couldn't steal the exact idea, but JT knew they always copied each other. He'd taken at least five of their prototypes and turned them into his own products. But failing to share information was punishable. By death.

Running the world was serious business, and only a handful of men like them were capable. Politicians were incompetent. And the power brokers at the table owned nearly all of them anyway.

A whooshing exhale escaped JT's mouth. The wind came with a sour stench from his lower intestines. A reverse fart. The downside to blocking his butt. He ignored the coughs and his colleagues' sickened expressions.

"Damn, JT, blow that wind in the other direction," McMahon said as he waved his cowboy hat in front of his face.

Discreetly, JT pulled out his mini R2D2 spray and spritzed a whiff of forest scent under the table. None of his fellow Society members deserved cover-up spray, however, because they shouldn't have forced him to share his latest invention.

JT wafted the scent toward himself. "I've developed a laser."

"And?" McMahon exclaimed a little too quickly.

JT hesitated. "We shoot the laser into the sky. If there's a spirit within the beam, they're disconnected from any human they're guiding."

"I don't get it," Moulder said.

JT stormtroopered more antacids into his mouth. While crunching, he said, "All that crap about guardian angels and deities and spirits? Seems it's all true."

Moulder sat back. "Fuck me."

"I feel the same way," JT said. He purposely forgot to mention his attempts at extracting and bottling their energy to sell. "That's why I haven't shared this yet. For the longest time, I didn't believe it. I'm still not sure I do."

"You're still not explaining what you're doing and what happens," said McMahon.

"These spirits help guide humans," JT continued. "They're all that peace and love crap religion's always talking about."

"Why do we care?" Moulder asked.

Gas bubbles of impatience fizzed inside JT. He squeezed his cheeks, another reverse fart of disgust ready to rip through the room. "Because those things help humans find themselves and all that shit. Like happiness from within. Woo-woo kind of rubbish."

"And?" Moulder asked.

JT turned to him. "Seriously?" He leaned forward, his hands firmly on the mahogany table. "Once people disconnect from all the hippy religious mumbo-jumbo crap, guess what? They're left with an emptiness, a hole inside." He looked around the table, slowly meeting each man eye to eye. "And guess how they fill that ache?" He put on his practiced evil Darth Vader–like smile, the kind the villain would have used if he could. "They buy stuff. *Our* stuff."

McMahon sat back and gave his unlit cigar a quick nibble. "Holy baby sons of guns."

"That's right," JT said. "Buying stuff makes them feel okay for a little while. But the emptiness inside always comes back. So they keep buying more until it becomes an addiction. Materialism becomes their new religion." He paused for effect, then added, "And we all make more money."

"You need to share with us," Wang said.

JT laughed. "No, I'm not sharing it."

He sat back and again smiled his villain grin. "You can hire my team, though. I'll even cut you a break." Joy spread across JT's face. Profiting off others in The Society made him especially gleeful.

"McMahon," Wang said. "He can't do that!"

"He can," said McMahon. "Our bylaws say we inform each other about what we're doing, but we don't have to share any details about trade secrets."

"Listen," JT said. "I'm helping all of us and increasing consumer demand everywhere. I'm making people want more stuff. We all benefit." Unsure if they were buying his bullshit, he added, "And this means we'll all become Big T's in the next couple of years."

A satisfied laugh filled the room. Power and ego always lifted insecure men's spirits.

Fuck all of you ran through JT's mind as he laughed along with them. The last thing he would do was help them—*he* would be the world's first trillionaire. He would rule them all.

Chapter Three

The rain stopped as the sun began to rise. After ten hours of driving through West Virginia, Pennsylvania, Ohio, Indiana, Illinois, and now Missouri, Alex had little left in her. As they passed St. Louis, she saw signs for the Mark Twain National Forest. They were getting close.

Crystal stirred next to her. She'd fallen into a deep sleep somewhere in Ohio, and Alex didn't want to disturb her. She preferred the silence anyway.

Crystal stretched her arms and began re-chewing the masticated gum she'd somehow stored in her mouth while sleeping. "We almost there?"

"Just a few more miles. Can you get the map out?"

They exited the interstate at the town of Bourbon. Crystal opened the paper and guided Alex to a rutted, unpaved road outside of town.

Crystal jumped and grabbed the dashboard. "Look out!"

Alex slowed down. "Deer." She scanned both sides of the road as she steered the car down a narrow dirt road to a rickety-looking wooden structure.

"I don't like this," she said, putting the car in park. Graying white paint peeled off the sides of the house, and the front steps sagged with the weight of countless previous owners and guests. "We're here because of a stranger. What if she's working with those SUV guys?"

Crystal looked at her. "Do we have a choice?"

Alex turned off the car. "Well, we'll find out soon enough."

Cautiously, they made their way to the front steps, but before they reached the porch, the front door opened. A lean and fit man of average height stood behind the flimsy screen door. He wore formfitting wraparound sunglasses that hid his eyes but not the energy from his intense stare. He had the scruffy remnants of a reddish brown and gray streaked beard, like he'd had a full face of hair once and couldn't completely give it up. His auburn hair sported a growing-out military buzz cut.

A tall, imposing woman brushed him aside and came to the screen, a beer bottle in one hand, an unlit cigarette in the other. "Don't worry about Hank. We just have to be careful." The bodyguard stepped aside as she opened the door with her elbow. "Come in."

Alex hesitated, her hair streaked anxious red and stress magenta, but Crystal nudged past her and walked inside. Alex followed. A woman who drank at eight in the morning couldn't be that bad.

A fire crackled in the fireplace. The interior was cabin rustic, with rough wood walls and floor. Handmade-looking pine furniture was scattered about the room. Patchwork quilts and cushions covered the sofa and chairs, making the place seem like a Midwest movie-set country home.

"It's gauche as all farts, but it's what we got." The woman pointed to the floral sofa and chairs. "Please, sit." She took the rocking chair by the fire. "I'm Jacqueline, but everyone calls me Jackie." She pointed her cigarette toward the figure leaning out the front door. "And that's Hank."

Hank shut the door and gave them a polite tilt of the head as he stood guard at the entranceway. He turned to Jackie. "Seems clear."

Jackie nodded.

Alex sat in an overstuffed armchair and studied the stranger in front of her. She had to be in her mid-forties, near Alex's age. Wrinkles had begun to etch her face, the start of a story Alex wanted to know. Her long, naturally wavy hair was streaked blonde, most likely a combination of the sun and a bottle. Her athletic body, grounded stance, and black cowboy boots made Alex think she'd grown up on a horse somewhere in the West, yet her black slim-fit jeans and black T-shirt looked designer casual, like an outfit an artist might wear. She also gave off the energy of someone who'd lived through rough times, making her an interesting contradiction.

Alex pointed to the pink-flowered sofa piled with pillows of all shapes and sizes. "That's Crystal. And I'm Alex." She stared at Jackie's bottle. "Do you always drink at eight a.m.?"

The bodyguard walked into the room. "Jackie worked in Vegas, so she never knows if it's day or night."

Jackie laughed and took a sip. "It's nonalcoholic. We've been up all night waiting and were getting worried." She nodded in Hank's direction. "Hank was ready to go find you." They looked at each other with amusement.

Crystal blew a bubble and popped it. "Nice to meet you."

"You knew we were coming?" Alex asked.

Jackie nodded. "Of course. We had people driving by and checking on you ever since West Virginia. The last tracker somehow lost you, so we were getting concerned."

Alex leaned forward, trying to fend off the sleep overtaking her. "What are we doing here?"

"Ah, good. Straight to the point." Jackie took a drag of her unlit cigarette and held it in the air. Nodding toward it, she said, "I'm trying to quit."

"Jackie." Hank motioned to the guests. "Would you like to offer them something to eat or drink?"

"Oh, shit, my manners. Sorry about that, ladies." Jackie put her cigarette away. "Can I get you anything?"

"Tea, if you have it," Crystal said.

Alex's head nodded forward as she struggled to keep her eyes open. "I'm too exhausted for anything."

Jackie stood. "Let me show you to a bedroom so you can get some rest. Join us later."

Alex struggled to get out of her chair. Being over-exhausted was like being drunk. She staggered after Jackie to a bedroom upstairs, where she took off her shoes, fell onto the bed, and drifted off immediately.

***

Alex woke to the late afternoon sun shining through the window. If she slept any longer, she knew she'd screw up her sleep schedule, so she forced herself to get up. She felt rested for the first time in months and noticed her hangover had gone away. They'd started lasting two or three days, but now that she was better, Alex looked forward to a drink or two. With all the stress she was under, quitting would have to wait a while.

Following the voices, she made her way downstairs. Crystal, Hank, and Jackie were sitting in the living room as flames crackled in the fireplace.

"Welcome back," Jackie said. "You were out like a light."

"Sorry," Alex said. "I drove all night and was beyond exhausted."

Jackie smiled. "No need to be sorry. We all got some sleep."

Alex joined the others and sat in an overstuffed armchair close to the fire. The warmth relaxed her.

"It's always cold in this room," Jackie said, pointing to the flames.

"It feels great," Alex said. She looked at the others. "Did I miss anything?"

Crystal cracked her gum. "We all crashed after you did and just came back down."

Jackie stood. "Before we talk, though, what can I get you to drink? I promised myself I'd remember my manners this time."

Alex smiled. "Do you have any alcohol?"

Jackie nodded. "Anything in particular?"

"Vodka perhaps? Or whiskey?" Alex ignored Crystal's gaze; she'd quit when she was ready.

"Sit," Hank told Jackie. "I'll get it."

Jackie nodded her thanks as Hank walked to the dining side of the room. "By the way," he said as he looked through the cupboards under the sink. "I made some chili earlier if you're hungry."

Jackie stood and shook her head. "I'm not a very good host, am I?" She motioned toward the dining table. "Let's all eat, and I'll fill you in on what I know."

Hank straightened and held up a bottle of Jack Daniels. "No vodka, but we've got whiskey."

"Perfect," Alex said as she walked to the table. "A large one, please."

They all sat. Hank opened the Jack and poured Alex a generous glass. He downed a quick shot himself and offered the bottle to Crystal, who shook her head. He placed the whiskey on the counter behind him as Alex reached over and picked up her drink.

Jackie filled their bowls and plates with chili, cornbread, and salad. She handed out the dishes as Hank passed around iced tea.

Alex downed her drink in two gulps. "Do you mind?" she asked Hank as she pointed toward the counter.

"Of course not." He picked up the Jack Daniels and passed it to Alex, who poured herself at least three shots' worth. She took a large gulp, grimacing slightly at the sour taste that filled her mouth and nostrils. She then topped up her drink and placed the bottle on the table in front of her.

Jackie laughed. "A woman after my own heart."

Alex swallowed another large gulp of the amber liquid and closed her eyes. The sweet warmth of alcohol coursed through her body and calmed her. Her muscles relaxed. The first two shots were always the best. This was her sweet spot; much more and she'd go into an all-out binge, but she didn't care. She poured more into her glass and kept it close, telling herself it was her last drink.

Jackie casually picked up the bottle and moved it away from her. "You okay?"

Alex nodded. "Now I am. This has been the most insane twenty-four hours of my life." She sat back. "And that's saying something." She looked at her glass. "Not only did I need a drink, I earned it after everything over the past day."

Jackie pointed toward Alex's plate. "Get some food in you."

Alex broke off a piece of corn bread. "Who are you guys?"

Jackie pointed to Hank. "Well, Hank here was Army Special Forces for years. He's retired now and helps protect people."

Hank stiffened.

Jackie smiled. "That's all we can say because he'd have to kill us if we knew any more."

Crystal laughed.

Alex looked at her. "I think she means it."

"Oh." Crystal sat back, surprise written across her face.

Hank took off his sunglasses, his piercing, ice-blue eyes resting on all of them one by one. "And Jackie, she worked in a Las Vegas casino as a card dealer and is also retired and protects people."

Jackie grinned. "In a slightly different way."

After they finished eating, Crystal reached for her iced tea. "Can I ask what's going on?"

Jackie glanced at Hank, who gave her a slight nod. She then looked at Alex and Crystal. "I'm a really direct person, so I'm going to say it straight out." She leaned toward the two women. "Crystal, you're not from here."

"From Missouri?" Alex asked with a half snort, her tongue loosening with the whiskey. "I could have told you that."

Jackie shook her head and looked from Alex to Crystal. "You're not from this planet. You're from another dimension."

"Oh, please, no." Alex knocked back another large gulp of whiskey, finishing the glass. Just when she thought it couldn't get worse.

Jackie turned to Alex and smiled. "Your friend here isn't human. She's a guiding spirit, like a guardian angel…but not."

"Oh, so she's not actually one," Alex remarked. "Didn't get her wings or something?"

Jackie pushed away her empty plate. "Angels never take human form. Crystal was a person like us, but she died and merged with the spirit side. She was helping guide people here on Earth, but something happened and now she's back in human form."

Alex straightened in her chair, her eyes finding the Jack. "Oh, come on." Thoughts were becoming more difficult.

Jackie turned back to Crystal. "Someone's disconnecting spirits from their energy and the person they're helping. They end up materializing here on earth."

Crystal blinked but said nothing.

Alex leaned over and grabbed the whiskey bottle. She shook her head as she sat, then poured herself another generous glass. "I lost my fiancé and my job. I probably can't go back to my apartment. Strange men are trying to kill me. And I'm with a bunch of strange people. This is so fucked up." She took two large swallows of alcohol and refilled her glass.

Jackie stood and took the bottle from Alex's hand. "That's it for you." She handed the whiskey to Hank, who nodded and put it on the floor between his legs.

The numbing effects of the booze settled into Alex's cells. Slowly, she slouched in the chair, her head bobbing forward ever so slightly. It felt so good. She focused as she tried to enunciate her words. "Look, I get aliens. I worked with a bunch of them twenty years ago, and I know there are dozens of alien species all around Earth. But spirits? *Spirits*? Beyond the grave, from other dimensions, not-of-this-universe, once-were-human spirits?" She shook her head. "No."

"I'm sorry for whatever happened to you," Jackie said. "And that you're bitter. But that doesn't mean I'm making this up."

Crystal looked at Alex. "I'm not sure. I know it sounds crazy, but I'm not surprised."

Alex snorted and shook her head, downing the rest of the Jack. A splash of whiskey backwashed into her mouth. She shouldn't have eaten so much dinner.

"Perhaps you disconnected yourself from something bigger than you," Jackie said.

Alex sank back against the chair, the familiar numbness taking over. She floated in serene stillness as she hoped for the sweet relief of passed-out sleep. She held out the glass she forgot she was clutching.

"No more," Jackie said. "You need to stop drinking. You know that. Start listening to yourself."

Alex chuckled. "Why? I followed my heart when I was younger and had it ripped in two. And it just happened again. It's not a good idea to listen to myself."

She closed her eyes and relaxed into the semi-consciousness that started to wrap her in a blackout hug.

"Alex," Jackie said, "you're not crazy. *We're* not crazy."

Eyes closed, Alex nodded sloppily. Now was a great time to pass out.

Jackie continued. "Alex, Crystal isn't the only one. There's a worldwide group helping spirits all over the world. That's why the woman at Cracker Barrel and the couple at the gas station helped you. They're part of our network."

Alex tried to wave Jackie away, but her arm flopped onto the kitchen table. It seemed to take less booze to get drunk these days.

"It's okay," Jackie replied. "Don't worry. About any of it. We're only here to help. Okay? Forget about the rest."

As Alex drifted into a mixture of exhaustion and velvet whiskey blackness, Hank pulled her up and walked her across the room. She let herself fall into the nothingness she longed for.

***

Alex landed back in her body with a thud. Her pounding heart was ready to explode. She groaned as the headache and nausea welcomed her back to the world. Another doozy of a hangover. They seemed to be getting worse with each passing month. She opened her eyes to the early-morning light spreading across the sky outside the window. Groaning again, she rolled over. The drinking really had to stop.

She had dreamt she was in her old NoHo condo, the one she'd thought she'd bought with Finn the Fuckhead. Memories flooded back, making her stomach turn. She leaned over and threw up into a trash can someone had strategically placed by the bed. Alex wiped her mouth with a tissue and lay back, closing her eyes and trying not to remember.

The day her future started to crumble, she was checking the pockets of clothes she was washing, making sure no miscellaneous items were left behind. When she stuck her hand into Finn's khakis, she pulled out a dirty G-string. The sexy purple-and-black underwear looked familiar, and Alex could no longer deny what she'd been suspecting.

She spun around and leaned against the washer, her hair streaked shock white. Hand over her chest, she struggled to breathe. She and a coworker, Maddie, worked out at the same soul cycle class every week. Alex remembered mentioning how pretty Maddie's panties and bra were when they were changing after class. Alex loved the purple with black accents and had asked Maddie where she'd gotten them.

"Oh, Madame Marie's," Maddie had said. "An amazing boutique in the West Village. They specialize in lingerie."

"Oh, wow," Alex said. "I send my fiancé there every Valentine's Day. I love that place."

This was it. Alex finally had to accept the reality that had faced her for months. Although she'd seen the looks between the two of them, she'd always pushed the truth aside. She'd seen them brush next to each other and had even seen Finn wink at Maddie once. But Alex always found an excuse because denial was so much safer.

She had to admit the truth that was clutched in her hands. Finn had bought the lingerie as a gift for Maddie. How could Alex be so stupid?

When she confronted Finn over dinner, he yelled at her, accusing her of being crazy. He thrust his finger at her as his face reddened with anger. "You really want that engagement ring, don't you? Pulling a stunt like this and claiming that underwear came from me."

"What are you talking about?" Alex said. "I pulled them out of your pocket a couple of hours ago."

Finn slammed his fist on the table. "You're lying."

Alex stood and moved to the other side of the room, her legs trembling. She hated when Finn got this way. She physically distanced herself from him, like her former therapist had taught her. He had never hit her, not unless they were playing a sex game, but she needed to be careful. Her father's anger had taught her that.

"Don't say that," she said through tears of anger and frustration. Her hair streaked all colors of emotion. "I know it's Maddie from the office. I've known for a while, but couldn't admit it."

"How stupid are you?" Finn yelled back. "They're not mine."

They argued for nearly an hour until Alex stepped back and gasped. It was so clear: Finn had been gaslighting her for years. Every suspicion Alex ever had, every wish she'd had for them as a couple, or even any thought she'd had…if it didn't suit Finn, he'd claim she was paranoid or making things up, or laugh at her and tell her she was crazy.

The first two years they were dating, before she moved in with him, he had love-bombed her. Wooed her, flattered her, made Alex feel like she was the most important person in the world. They went on exciting, extravagant dates: helicopter rides around Manhattan, the Caribbean for a quick tan, Paris for the weekend.

But once they moved in together, things changed. The insults and criticisms were subtle at first, so Alex easily brushed them aside. She could be too sensitive. Her mother had drilled that into her for as long as she could remember. But as the sex became rougher and the insults more vicious, Alex began to wonder what was wrong with her.

If Finn didn't like what she said, he told her she was wrong or stupid. Alex second-guessed herself, even when she knew she was right. And she always ended up agreeing with him. She had been willing to sacrifice her sanity and true self to have a husband and a baby. In her twenties, she had hope and a lot of time, but when she was forty, she realized she was losing her chances for a child. And now, at age forty-five, she was sure Finn was her last chance for the family her parents and society told her she needed in order to be happy. And normal.

She remembered what her therapist had told her. With all her might, Alex threw her shoulders back and stared directly into her fiancé's eyes.

Finn looked at her and stepped back. Alex could tell he saw her truth. He saw she'd figured him out, so his game was over. His eyes hardened to steel. "Fine. You're right. They are Maddie's. Does that make you happy?"

Alex's legs buckled, and she crumpled into a chair. She was sitting, but she was outside herself, looking down. She remembered this feeling from when she was young, when her father and mother had yelled at each other about his affairs. Alex had the horrifying epiphany she'd been trying to marry her father.

She couldn't look at Finn. No words would come out.

"Well," he said as he sat across from her, his voice getting colder by the word. "What do you want?"

Alex choked back a sob and caught her breath. "I want the truth. You've slept around, and I let it go. But you're having an affair with her. She's been acting weird toward me for months. I don't know if it's guilt or something sick she's playing at."

Finn laughed and looked her directly in the eye. "It's certainly not guilt."

Alex fell deeper inside her head. She heard herself say, "You need to leave."

Finn pushed back his chair and stood up. He walked toward her. "This is my house. My name's on the contract, not yours. Only mine." A wicked grin of satisfaction spread across his face. "I made sure of that."

Alex gasped. He had repeatedly assured her that both names were on the purchase agreement. That with electronic contracts, he only had to type in her signature. But she'd never seen the papers. He'd raised such a fuss when she asked about having a copy that she'd let it go.

Finn narrowed his eyes. "I want you gone by eight." He leaned into her face. "Tonight."

Alex's mouth dropped open. She couldn't think. He was kicking her out, but to where? She lived there.

Finn started toward the hall but turned back. Spite danced in his eyes. "And I'm keeping the dog. My name's on her adoption papers, not yours." He straightened and spat out his last words. "Leave. I never wanted to marry you." He turned on his heel and disappeared through the doorway.

Alex stared at the empty space. She heaved and vomited her broken heart across the floor, leaving behind shattered dreams and lost hope. She shook her head. How could this be happening? In less than an hour, she'd lost her fiancé, her dog, her house, and her supposed friend.

She'd also lose her job. Finn and Maddie wouldn't want her in the office. And sure enough, three months later, right after the hugely successful, ground-breaking creative conference she'd been planning ended, she was fired from Finn's company, Klein Strategies. Alex hated herself for thinking hard work and success would give her job security. Deceit and manipulation had won out in the end.

Alex rolled over in the floral-blanketed bed in the dilapidated house somewhere in Missouri. She buried her face in the pillow, trying to forget the painful memories that looped endlessly in her head. All she wanted was to forget Finn. Her eyes became wet.

The knock on the bedroom door startled her. Quickly, she brushed off a tear sliding down her cheek.

"Alex, breakfast's ready. We're in the kitchen."

Crystal's footsteps faded down the stairs.

Alex carefully sat up and put her legs over the side of the bed. When the dizziness and nausea subsided, she stood and shakily put on her clothes.

She followed the sounds of breakfast and gingerly made her way to the kitchen. Jackie and Crystal were at the table while Hank busied himself at the stove. Alex sat and looked at the pint of water and three ibuprofen in front of her.

She looked up as Jackie smiled at her.

"Breakfast of champions." Jackie shrugged. "I've been there."

Alex gratefully downed the water and tablets.

Hank placed plates of scrambled eggs, bacon, potatoes, and toast in front of Alex, Crystal, and Jackie. Alex noticed his scruff was sprouting into a beard.

She covered her mouth as she gagged. Ever since her breakup with Finn, her stomach hadn't been the same.

"Thank you," said the others.

Hank nodded and joined them at the table. "My guilty pleasure." He poured hot sauce over his meal and dug into the mountain of food he'd made for himself.

Alex did her best to get some eggs and dry toast in her, but her stomach revolted. The smell alone made her gag. She pushed her plate away and turned to Jackie. "What's going on? I didn't understand what you were saying last night."

Jackie put down her fork and leaned back. "You sure? You didn't take it too well."

Alex nodded. "Yeah. I'm stuck here, aren't I?"

Jackie gave her a curious look. "No one's stuck here, Alex. You can walk out the door whenever you want. You're not a prisoner."

Alex nodded and lowered her head. She might not be Jackie's prisoner, but she definitely felt trapped. She had nowhere to go. Sour alcohol acid swam in her stomach. Her hair must have turned completely green because a bucket appeared under her chin. She emptied more of the pain of her nightmares into the plastic pail. A napkin wiped her mouth and the strand of ill-green hair that had gotten in the way.

Alex kept her eyes trained on the floor. "Sorry," she mumbled.

Jackie took the pail into another room. Alex heard breakfast plates being pushed aside.

She glanced up and saw Hank clearing the table. "Really sorry," she said.

"We all have demons," Hank said softly as he carried a pile of dishes to the sink.

Jackie sat down next to her. "I've been there. It's okay."

"I ruin everything," Alex said. Her life was turning into humiliation after humiliation.

Jackie sighed. "No, you don't. Anyway, we were finished."

Alex looked in her direction, but avoided her eyes. "I'd still like to know what's happening."

Jackie patted her arm. "I've only been told so much. We keep it that way in case we're captured. But there are people who want Crystal."

"Who? And why?"

Jackie sipped her tea. "I'm not sure. It's something to do with Crystal's energy. From what I understand, they want the energy but not the spirit that fell to Earth, so there's a problem with what they're doing. They need her so they can figure out what's wrong."

"Well, at least it's not Finn after me," Alex mumbled.

"The people chasing you and Crystal are kidnapping the spirits they find, and we're trying to stop them. We have safe houses set up around the world to hide them. You're in one now."

"How many people are part of this?" Alex asked.

"Of helping spirits?"

Alex nodded.

"Thousands at this point. Probably more."

"How many spirits have you found?" Crystal asked.

Jackie pulled out an unlit cigarette and took a drag. "That's the funny thing. People have found them, and some made it to safe houses, but they disappeared within a few weeks." She looked at Hank.

"That's my understanding," he said, clearing the last of the plates from the table. "We think the kidnappers are taking them in the middle of the night, but we're not sure. All we know is they're vanishing."

"How did it all start?" Crystal asked, a fresh stick of gum in her mouth. She offered the pack around the table.

Alex nodded and pulled out a stick of mint gum. Hopefully, it would mask the vomit aftertaste in her mouth.

Jackie dabbed her lips with her napkin, then placed it on the table. "This all started less than two years ago, I'd say. I'm not sure of the exact timing. But my understanding is some Buddhist monks in Nepal started feeling a disruption in the energy that makes up the universe."

Alex rolled her eyes but kept her mouth shut. She focused on getting as much flavor from the gum as she could.

Jackie held up her unlit cigarette and looked at her. "You can believe what you want, but science and quantum physics are proving all this. Those supposedly backward monks meditating in caves thousands of years ago understood much more than we do today."

Alex lightly snorted and mumbled, "May the force be with you." She knew arguing with delusional people was pointless, so she stayed quiet. Finn had taught her that.

"Monks discovered the spirits?" Crystal asked.

Plates clattered as Hank filled the dishwasher.

"Hank, what have you been told?" Jackie called over.

He straightened up, a dish towel across his shoulder. "I was in the Himalayas when this started. There were researchers in Nepal studying meditation in monks. Monks told the people leading the study something was wrong. They weren't sure what, but something wasn't right. The scientists contacted colleagues and they figured out what was happening."

"Who figured it out?" Crystal asked.

"The monks and some scientists." Hank shrugged. "I don't know exactly who."

"Seriously?" said Alex. "This sounds more like a movie than reality."

Hank grabbed the towel from his shoulder and dried his hands. He tossed the dish cloth onto the counter. He then leaned back and looked at Alex, his arms crossed. "I probably wouldn't believe any of this myself, except I was there. I've seen too much to doubt it."

"I didn't know that," Jackie said.

Hank gave her a quick wink. "Well, you know, if I tell you too much I'd have to eliminate you."

Jackie turned to Alex. "Billions of people believe there's more to life than what we see."

"They're zealots," Alex replied. "There's nothing more than us humans and a bunch of aliens all trying to make as much money as possible, all while screwing each other over."

Jackie leaned back and shook her head slightly, taking another unlit drag. "Have you ever seen The Dalai Lama? Seen him speak or anything?"

Alex fought the urge to roll her eyes again. "No. I stay away from men in dresses who claim to be holy."

Jackie's eyes widened. "Wow. Someone must have seriously hurt you."

"That has nothing to do with my beliefs."

"No faith, no hope." Jackie leaned back. "They're related."

Alex looked across the kitchen, hoping to find the whiskey. Her beliefs swam in a bottle of eighty proof.

Crystal cracked her gum. "Well, I believe you."

Jackie continued. "There's not much else. Like Hank said, some monks and scientists discovered what was happening. Once they realized spirits were falling to earth as humans, then disappearing, they secretly and quietly spread word through sanghas and Buddhist groups. They didn't know when or where a fallen spirit would show up."

Jackie reached for her pack of American Spirits and put her cigarette away. "Everyone took vows not to share what was happening, so the Spiritual Enterprise Network—or SEN, as it's also called—was born. We're trying to get the spirits back where they belong. And stop whoever or whatever's taking their energy."

Alex remained silent as angry black streaks mixed with the ill green. Since her hangover-foggy brain couldn't fully digest what Jackie was saying, she pushed it aside. Too much thinking never helped.

After they finished their tea and coffee, Hank put the mugs in the sink.

Jackie looked at Alex and Crystal. "You need to get going. Hank will go with you."

"We don't need a babysitter," Alex said. "I can drive."

Jackie shook her head. "It's too dangerous. He's going with you."

Hank sprinted across the room to the front window. "Shit, they're here," he said, grabbing his gun from the shelf by the front door.

"I don't hear anything," Jackie said.

"Get them out." Hank held his gun with both hands and stared out the window.

Jackie leapt from her chair. She pulled a small notebook from a kitchen drawer and opened her phone. She hastily scribbled on a piece of paper and shoved it toward Alex. "Hide this on you. In case we don't catch up with you, call this number when you arrive."

Alex handed the paper to Crystal, who tucked it into her bra.

Jackie rushed toward Hank and grabbed a set of keys hanging next to the door. "Drive the white Subaru Crosstrek," she said, tossing the keys to Alex. "Don't take the other car, only that one. It's filled and ready to go. Maps are in there."

Alex nodded.

Jackie turned toward the counter and took the lid off a ceramic owl cookie jar. She reached in and pulled out a gun. "There's a door in the back den. We'll draw them in here, so run out when they're inside. Head west."

Alex stayed rooted to her spot, eyes wide-open.

Jackie bent toward her, her body electric with anxiety. "This isn't a drill. Take Crystal and go. *Now.*"

Crystal grabbed Alex's arm. "Come on."

The two rushed into the back room of the house as someone kicked in the front door. A shot rang out as sounds of punching and grunting filled their ears.

Crystal unlocked the door and pulled Alex out of the house. She turned Alex toward her and shook her hard. "Alex, come back."

Alex blinked and looked at her. She gasped and said, "I'm here. I'm here." She pressed the fob twice and opened both car doors.

Both women looked right and left, making sure no one was outside. Alex heard the sounds of furniture breaking and Jackie's screams.

Crystal tugged on Alex's arm. "Come on."

The women ran to the Subaru and jumped in. In one motion, Alex started the car and put it in drive. She sped away from the house, flinching as she heard the front window shatter. She looked in her rearview mirror and saw Hank falling outside to the ground.

Alex rushed down the road. She turned west on Interstate 44 and headed toward Oklahoma. "Get the maps out. And that slip of paper. Let's figure out where we're going."

Crystal opened the glove compartment and pulled out a handful of maps.

Alex glanced over, her hands shaking on the steering wheel. "Are there sunglasses anywhere?"

Crystal rummaged through the papers and shook her head. "No, sorry." She glanced down to her left. "Wait." She opened the top of the elbow rest between the two of them and pulled out two pairs of Ray-Ban Wayfarers.

"Ta-da." Crystal handed a pair to Alex.

Alex took the glasses and put them on.

Crystal laughed and put on the second pair. "We're the Blues Sisters."

Alex focused on the road. "Now's not the time to be funny. Get that slip of paper so we can find out where we're going."

Crystal reached into her bra. "Oh, shoot," she said as she searched around. "Shoot, shoot, shoot."

"Don't tell me you lost the address."

Crystal reached deep inside her bra and pulled out the piece of paper, then sighed. "Got it." She looked at the note. "So," she said, "it says Sedona, and there's a phone number."

Alex gripped the steering wheel. "Fuck. Not Sedona."

"Why not?"

Alex shook her head. "Doesn't matter." She stared at the highway in front of them. "Last place I want to go." She sighed. "Fuck it."

Crystal opened the maps for Oklahoma and New Mexico. She lost herself behind a sea of paper and crumpling noises. After finding the Arizona map, she looked it over. "We should drive as fast as we can through

Oklahoma, then shoot straight through New Mexico and Arizona on the freeway." She refolded the map. "There aren't many road choices."

With a nod, Alex pressed the accelerator. Her chest tightened, a warning she was on the verge of a panic attack. Strands of anxious red and stress magenta swung in front of her eyes.

After they left Oklahoma City and picked up Interstate 40, a dark anxiety grew inside Alex's hangover. She kept looking in her rearview mirror. It started as a small dot far behind them on the somewhat-empty road, but it slowly got bigger. She gasped when she realized the car looked like the black SUV they'd seen at the house earlier that morning; it was weaving in and out of traffic at high speed. And gaining quickly.

Alex stepped on the gas. "This isn't good."

"What's happening?"

"I think they found us," she said as she passed an oversized cargo truck going more than ninety miles an hour.

"Wait," Crystal said. "It could be someone in a hurry. Let's drive normally and not make ourselves so obvious."

Alex couldn't think through her panic and hangover. She peered in the mirror again. "That's more than someone in a hurry. That's someone on a mission." She glanced at Crystal. "It doesn't matter. They're gaining so fast we can't outrun them." She looked at the road in front of them as her heart pounded.

Within minutes, the SUV was on their bumper. It swerved into the left lane and drove next to them. Alex tried to speed up, but the car matched her. She braked quickly, but the SUV followed suit. The windows were blacked out, so she couldn't see inside.

From the corner of her eye, she saw the backseat window roll down. Crystal screamed. "*No!*"

Alex jumped and glanced to her left as the SUV accelerated and began to pass them. Jackie's bloody face hung out the SUV's open window.

"*No!*" she echoed.

A gun appeared from behind Jackie and was placed against her temple. Alex rolled down her window.

"No," Jackie croaked through bloodied teeth and shook her head.

Jackie fell back out of sight.

Alex gripped the steering wheel even harder.

The SUV slowed slightly, so the passenger window was again parallel with Alex. A figure in a black ski mask leaned out the open window and yelled over the sound of the wind, "Follow us or she dies. Slowly and painfully."

The figure disappeared into the dark as the blacked-out window closed.

Alex's hands shook violently as she tried to keep up with the SUV.

Crystal helped steady the wheel. "Get behind them and follow them. We can't outrun them." She glared at Alex. "We have no choice. Do it!"

Alex slowed down as the SUV merged into the right lane in front of them. She followed the car for several miles to a Phillips 66 in Weatherford. They drove past the gas station and food court to the back of the property. Several eighteen wheelers were dotted around the sizable parking area, but they all looked empty. "There might be help here."

"Or not," Crystal said as they moved farther away from the trucks. They crossed a road and entered what looked like an abandoned dirt lot.

The SUV parked behind a metal building. Alex pulled in near the car but far enough away that she might have a chance at escape.

A ski-masked figure jumped out. He looked like a champion bodybuilder, his arms so thick and muscular Alex wondered if he could put them down by his sides.

He opened his back door. Jackie was bent over semiconscious, her hands tied. Another military type sat next to her, a gun in his lap.

Alex stepped out of the car, unsure of what to say. "What's this all about, sir? We're on a girls' trip."

"Shut up," was the reply.

The hulk approached Alex as his colleague scrambled out the back. Jackie slumped over, blood matting her hair.

The second military figure walked around the car and pointed his gun at Crystal, who was still sitting in her seat. "You. Get out."

Alex turned to him. "Why do you want her?"

The militia-looking brute backhanded Alex with his gun. "I said shut up."

She fell to the ground. Alex heard the ringing in her ears more than she felt the pain. Her jaw was going to hurt. Tears stung her eyes from the force of the blow. She threw up what little she had in her stomach.

Slowly, Alex sat up and watched as Crystal got out of the car, her hands in the air, her mouth still cracking gum. Two military figures grabbed her. One jabbed a needle in her neck while the other put his arm around her waist. In one movement, he picked her up and carried her to the SUV. Alex saw him toss Crystal in the back, next to Jackie.

The back door slammed shut. Alex got to her knees as the SUV's engine roared to life and sped away. Carefully, she stood, fighting her dizziness and nausea. As she straightened, the back door of the SUV opened, and Jackie fell to the ground.

"No! Jackie!" Alex staggered toward her, falling twice and scraping her knees along the way. As she got next to Jackie, Alex asked, "Are you okay?"

Jackie rolled onto her back and groaned. "I'll be fine. Help me up."

Alex pulled her into a sitting position. She grabbed the zip tie on Jackie's wrists and untwisted enough of the binding so Jackie could free herself. She put her hands under Jackie's arms and helped her to her feet. They both staggered to the Crosstrek.

"What happened?" Alex asked as they got in.

"It was nasty, but we thought we'd given you enough time to get away." She turned to Alex. "Sorry about that."

"What are you talking about? I thought you were both dead. How did they find us?"

"From what little I overheard, they used satellite imaging. I guess our team couldn't stop them." Jackie pulled a tissue from her pocket and wiped some of the blood off her face. "We have to get to headquarters."

"You need help," Alex said.

Jackie smiled wryly. "My ex-boyfriends have done worse." She put on her seat belt. "We have to find Crystal."

Alex turned the Subaru toward the gas station store. "Not before I get you some first-aid supplies."

She rushed inside and returned with alcohol, ointment, bandages, and a large bottle of ibuprofen. She also carried four Vitamin Waters: one for Jackie, two for her hangover, and one extra, just in case. She then helped Jackie clean herself and gave them both several ibuprofen.

"How do we find Crystal?" Alex asked as she opened the sugary drink. She took a long swig and pressed the cool bottle against her aching jaw.

Jackie cleaned her wounds as best she could. "I've no clue where they're taking her, so let's get to Sedona."

Alex shifted into drive and headed toward the gas pumps. "What about Hank? How's he?"

Jackie's eyes watered. "I don't know. I'm assuming he was unconscious when they took me and left. I can't think about the other possibility."

Alex wasn't convinced Hank was alive. "Are you sure you're okay?" she asked as she stopped in front of a gas pump. "I'm sure we could find a hospital or walk-in clinic nearby."

"Let's drive for a bit and see how I am in a few hours."

Alex agreed, then hopped out and quickly filled the tank. When she got back in, she said, "If you get faint or anything, though, tell me. I'll take you to an emergency room."

Jackie nodded. "Let's head to Sedona. Gather and figure out a plan."

"Should we call them?"

"Well, we can't," Jackie said. "We don't have phones. Unless you have one?"

Alex shook her head. "It's crushed on a highway somewhere in West Virginia." She started the car and headed toward the interstate. "At least we have somewhere to go." She saw Jackie reach for the maps. "Don't worry about that," Alex said. "We'll stay on 40 until Flagstaff, which is hours away. And I know the way from there. Get some rest."

Alex pressed the accelerator to the floor, her hangover left on the pavement at the rest stop. As much as she dreaded it, getting to Sedona was all that mattered.

Chapter Four

Crystal opened her eyes and slowly sat up on the cold floor, her body aching. Shivering, she wrapped her biker jacket tightly around her.

The concrete cell measured no more than ten feet by ten feet. It was painted military green, with no windows and no light, except one glaring fluorescent bulb hanging from the concrete ceiling. A cot sagged against the wall, a dark green bristly looking blanket thrown over it. In the far corner sat a black, five-gallon steel bucket with a cover. A roll of paper towels lay next to it.

Crystal shakily stood as she tried to remember what had happened. She fumbled through her leather jacket and found her gum, then popped in a stick to cover the sour taste in her mouth.

She sat on the edge of the cot. As much as she tried, Crystal only remembered the past few months, but they were hazy, like she'd been flickering in and out of consciousness. Her first solid memory was sitting in a dirt lot in Jersey City not long before she met Alex.

Alex and the past couple of days were all she could remember about herself, though she recognized objects, places, and things. She could even remember world history, but she couldn't remember her own. And she seemed human, not like a spirit or an angel. Not that she understood how that felt.

She tensed as she heard the beeping of a keypad.

Another military type entered and roughly grabbed her by the arm. Crystal looked into his ice-cold eyes. There was nothing. He lifted her off the cot and half dragged her down the hall before pushing her into another room and slamming the door shut.

Crystal looked around. A gray steel table with four uncomfortable-looking metal chairs sat in the middle of the room. The same type of fluorescent bulb hung from the ceiling. She headed to the table and crumpled into a seat. The coldness of the chair startled her.

The door opened. A disheveled older man in a white lab coat strode in, a large crooked nose leading the way. Noisily, he dropped a stack of folders on the table and sat down, his curly white hair bouncing around above his head but glued motionless near his scalp. He looked like he was wearing a mushroom cloud. The stranger glanced at Crystal and smiled a doctor's smile, somewhat warm yet mostly clinical.

"Well, who do we have here?" The lab-coated man opened the top folder and read the paper inside. He shook his head and closed the file, putting it aside. He then opened the second folder and clucked as he shook his head again.

He shuffled through the papers, opening and closing file after file and shaking his head. He grabbed a pen from his front pocket and made notes while mumbling to himself.

Crystal blew a small bubble and popped it with a loud crack.

The peculiar-looking man jumped. He looked at her, confusion clouding his face. "Oh. Oh, dear," he said, closing his latest folder. He smiled sheepishly. "I always get lost in my work." He shuffled through the pile and pulled out the bottom file.

"Here we are," he said, opening it. He glanced at the paper inside, then toward Crystal. "I'm Dr. Maximilian Underhill, but everyone calls me Dr. Max. Or Max, if you prefer."

"Well, Max," Crystal said as she continued to crack her gum, "what am I doing here? And who are you?"

Dr. Max chuckled and tried to run his hand through his hair. He yelped as his fingers stuck to his head.

Crystal watched with amusement as he tried to unglue his fingers from his stiff, unruly mess. He yanked himself free with another small yelp.

"Like I said, I'm Dr. Max. I'm a doctor and a scientist, and I'm running the study here."

"What study?"

He busied himself trying to unstick his fingers from each other, then glanced up. "Of course you wouldn't remember. You have amnesia. That's why you're here." He pried his fingers apart and picked up his pen. "So where do you come from?"

Crystal cracked her gum and shoved her hands into her biker jacket pockets. "I'm not exactly sure. Missouri possibly?"

The lab-coated man looked up, surprised. "That's where were you born?"

"Oh. Where do I come from? I thought you said where *did* I come from." Crystal looked at the wall behind him. Where was she born? She searched her memory but came up blank. "I don't know," she finally replied.

"Hmm," the man said. "I figured as much." He made a note on the paper. "Do you remember your name?"

Crystal searched her memory. "Not my real name. But everyone calls me Crystal."

He nodded and made another note. "Tell me anything you remember."

After a slight pause, she said, "There's not much. The furthest back I clearly remember is a few days ago. I was wandering around New Jersey.

And everything was so new. I couldn't remember anything—not my name, where I lived, nothing. And now I'm here."

"Hmm, I see." Dr. Max made a few notes, then looked back at her. "Anything else you remember?"

Crystal shrugged. "No. I mean, a woman helped me and tried to figure out where I live. And horrible men showed up, beat a person I was with, and kidnapped me. And now I'm here."

"Oh, tsk, tsk," Dr. Max said with distracted impatience. "Nobody kidnapped you. You're here so we can help you."

"Help me with what?"

The scientist looked up. "Like I said, you lost your memory. I'm working on ways to help people with amnesia. You probably don't remember because of your condition, but you're part of a huge study we're doing."

Crystal cocked her head to one side. "How many amnesia patients have been here?"

"Quite a few actually." Dr. Max reached across the table and patted her hand. "Don't worry about anyone else. I'm here to help you."

Crystal pulled her hand away. There were other fallen spirits like her. And they'd been caught and brought to wherever she was. But where was that?

Dr. Max made a few more notes, then closed his folder and stood. Before leaving, he turned around. "We'll start tests on you tomorrow, so get as much sleep as you can."

"Tell me why you kidnapped me," Crystal yelled as the door locked shut behind him.

***

Alex kept her eyes glued to the road as she weaved in and out of eighteen-wheelers on Interstate 40. They'd made it into New Mexico and through Albuquerque, but the sun had gone down a couple of hours earlier. As much as she loved being on the road, she found heavy truck traffic and driving after dark becoming more and more difficult as each year went by.

Alex felt herself getting tired. She'd been on the road at least eight hours and knew she had six or so left to go, but she was nodding off. At least seeing Jackie sleep was good.

Alex gasped. Or maybe it wasn't. Jackie could be seriously injured, have a concussion, or even worse. What if she had a brain bleed? Should Alex have kept her awake like they did in TV shows?

"Damn," Alex said, then looked at her passenger. "Jackie. You okay?"

Jackie remained motionless.

Alex's hair streaked stress magenta. She raised her voice. "Jackie. Wake up."

Jackie's arm moved.

"Jackie!"

Alex let out a long exhale when Jackie's eyes opened.

"Where am I?" she started.

"Sorry," Alex said. "I was afraid you had brain damage or something."

With a groan, Jackie straightened up. "Killer headache, but I'm fine." She gently touched her jaw. "And my jaw hurts like hell. But I'll be okay. How are you doing?"

Alex shrugged. "My face aches from where I got smacked, but I'm okay." She glanced at Jackie. "My ex liked to play rough also, so I'm used to it."

Jackie nodded. "I hear you."

Alex's steely grip on the wheel relaxed into a general white-knuckle hold. "I'm exhausted. I don't think I can make it to Sedona."

"Don't even try." Jackie pointed into the distance. "I see lights ahead, so there must be somewhere we can stop."

Alex nodded, fighting the urge to close her eyes.

"Roll down the windows," Jackie said.

The cold desert air rushed through the car. It helped, but Alex was sliding down inside herself. Sleep would feel so good. If she could just shut her eyes for a few minutes...

The punch to her arm brought her attention back to the road.

Jackie pointed to the exit coming toward them. "Get off here. There's a Flying J where we can rest."

Alex fought to stay awake and drive in a straight line. She pulled into the truck stop and parked near enough to the travel center for safety but not too close. She put her seat back and immediately fell asleep.

They woke as the sun rose and were back on the road by seven.

"You okay to drive?" Jackie asked.

Alex nodded as she merged back onto the interstate. "I wouldn't have made it last night." She sipped the coffee they'd gotten at the truck stop. "But I'm tons better now. You're looking rather black and blue, though. How are you?"

Jackie sipped her drink. "Well, my face is killing me and I ache all over, but I'm sure nothing's broken." She smiled. "So, it's a good day."

Alex couldn't help but smile back. "Maybe we should celebrate with some ibuprofen. My jaw really hurts."

They both downed a couple of tablets. "How can we find Crystal?" Alex asked.

Jackie stretched and groaned. "I'm sure Hank's found her by now." She glanced at Alex. "Even though I'm sure no one's tracking us because they have Crystal, we should wait until headquarters to talk about her."

Alex shook her head. "You really think people are tracking you?"

Jackie nodded. "Sometimes. Satellites can hear almost anything these days. We have to be careful."

"And this headquarters is different?"

Jackie nodded. "They can jam any signal trying to get in."

"You realize you sound like a conspiracist, yes?"

Jackie shrugged. "How do you think those men found you at the house?"

Alex didn't reply.

"Hank has orders to make sure Crystal's safe, no matter what. I don't matter. Sorry to say, you aren't top priority either. Her safety is his only job. And, trust me, Hank's trained to take his work seriously."

Alex remained silent but wondered again if he was still alive. His body had looked lifeless as it came crashing through the window. She gazed at the wide-open expanse in front of her. On one side, she saw flat desert as far as the horizon. Cliffs of red rock towered above the ground on the other. From nowhere, a thought popped into Alex's head. A drink, that's what she wanted. Going back to Sedona, where her heart had been ripped apart, wouldn't be easy.

"It's funny," Jackie said, looking out the window at the morning light on the red rocks. "New Mexico. Parts of Arizona. Southern Utah. They're the most beautiful, spiritual places in the country, yet few people ever visit beyond Santa Fe or Sedona. But this place is magical."

Spirit. Magic. Whatever. All life had given Alex was loss and assholes. Good name for a band. Loss and Assholes. She continued to weave in and out of the eighteen-wheelers clogging the highway. Why they tried to pass each other while going uphill boggled Alex's mind. One truck could cause a mile-long backup as it inched its way up a hill in the left lane, slowly passing another vehicle.

As they came into Flagstaff and started toward Interstate 17, Jackie motioned for Alex to get off. Alex nodded and drove onto a smaller highway lined with pine trees. She emerged from the trees and gasped. She'd forgotten how beautiful the drive into Oak Creek Canyon was.

A vast valley spread out over two thousand feet beneath her. She slowed to twenty-five as the narrow mountain road zigzagged down the massive cliff. Large outcrops of rock and pine trees hugged them on either side. The turns were nearly 180 degrees, so Alex slowed to nearly a crawl. Every so often she got a glimpse of the green pine. This was also her favorite way in and out of Sedona.

When they evened out at the bottom, Jackie laughed. "Welcome to Oak Creek Canyon."

Alex's body buzzed as they made their way down the road. When they turned a corner, she marveled at the natural beauty. Red rock cliffs rose above her, their burnt orange and red colors creating a stunning contrast to the deep-blue sky.

"I love coming in this way," Jackie said.

Alex nodded. "I forgot how gorgeous it is here." She soaked in the red rock beauty. After her breakup in Sedona and realizing the only other place she had friends was New York City, she'd settled back in the East Village in Manhattan. Some days, when the light was just right, she'd marvel at how the sun caught the brick buildings and lit them up like the red rocks in Arizona and Utah. But after ten years of stress in the only city she thought mattered, Alex had forgotten how drawn she was to the Southwest. If Skeater hadn't fucked her over, she probably wouldn't have left.

"Do you have the phone number?" Jackie asked.

"Oh, shoot," Alex replied. "I'm not sure where the paper is."

Jackie sat up straight. "Do you think Crystal had it when they took her?"

"I don't know. Crystal had it in her bra, but she took it out. I'm not sure where she put it."

"Okay," Jackie said. "But we have to find it. Or headquarters will have to move."

"Crap." Alex fumbled through her pockets, but they were empty. She felt around as much as she could on the car floor while keeping her eyes on the road. Just some sandy dirt. She reached over and opened the glove compartment.

Jackie sighed with relief when she saw the note.

"What did you write?" Alex asked.

"It's a phone number. Glad I gave you this before you left because I don't have it memorized. The person answering will give us a public location to meet them. It changes all the time."

Jackie directed Alex through town until they found a phone store on the western side. Soon they were back in the car with a burner and an iPhone each.

Jackie held up the burner. "We'll connect with each other on these. Never call someone in the network on your iPhone because they're traceable. Burners aren't."

Alex nodded. "And the iPhone?"

"Make calls to us on the burner. You can Google, download apps, and do everything else on the iPhone, as long as it's not related to our work. You can call people also, but not anyone in the network." Jackie paused for a moment, then added, "Oh, and don't use the GPS on the regular phone if you're doing anything related to the underground. Use old-school paper maps instead."

"Don't really see the point of the iPhone," Alex mumbled.

"Excuse me?"

"Nothing. I heard you." Alex held both phones as she looked for somewhere to put them. "I probably need a handbag or something." She dropped them into the car door pocket next to her.

Jackie opened the slip of paper and dialed the number on it. She placed the phone to her ear. "Hi. It's Jackie. 515." She scribbled on the piece of paper. "Thanks. We'll be right there."

"What's with the number?" Alex asked as Jackie ended the call.

"My identification number. If we don't use it, we assume the person on the other end is an imposter."

"But Crystal and I didn't have one."

"Good point. Didn't think about that. But they were waiting for your call." Jackie directed Alex to a tourist information center, one of many that were fronts for timeshare sales. When they walked through the door, a short, round woman in her early seventies greeted them. She sported gray-streaked white hair and wore a brightly colored orange-and-pink muumuu. Her golden amber eyes radiated a warmth that wrapped around Alex.

"You made it in one piece," she said cheerfully.

Jackie threw her arms in the air. "Prickly," she called out.

"Pears," replied the older woman as she came out from behind the counter.

The two women embraced tightly.

"So great to see you, Jackie," the stranger said as she let go. "It's been forever."

"You too, Sharlene."

Sharlene gently touched Jackie's cheek; Jackie winced. "Sweetheart, what in the world happened?" She brushed back some hair on the side of Jackie's head. "You've got blood all over you."

Jackie stepped back. "I'm fine. It's Crystal we have to worry about. I got beat around a bit, but that doesn't matter. They got Crystal."

"What happened?"

"Hitmen came to the house right before Alex and Crystal left. Hank and I held them off to give the two a chance to escape, but the gunmen abducted me and caught up with Alex and Crystal." Jackie hung her head. "I'm so sorry. I didn't want them to trade me for her."

"Oh, shush, honey," Sharlene said. "I'm sure there was no choice."

"There wasn't," Alex said.

Jackie broke away from Sharlene. "Sorry. My manners again." She turned to Alex. "Alex, this is Sharlene. She's head of the Spiritual Enterprise Network I told you about."

Alex watched Sharlene blush. "Not head, honey. We're all equal in this network. I'm just trying to help a few kindred spirits."

Jackie quietly shook her head and mouthed "no" behind Sharlene, making clear to Alex that Sharlene was the group leader.

Alex held out her hand. "Great to meet you."

"Oh, no, we don't greet that way." Sharlene walked over and gave Alex a grandmother hug, the kind that says everything will be all right. Alex's hair turned bright pink as she surprised herself and rested in the embrace.

She stepped back as Sharlene released her. "What was that prickly pear thing you just did?"

Sharlene laughed. "Oh, just something silly between Jackie and me. One of us tried to harvest the plant in a national forest and almost got themselves a huge fine."

Jackie smiled. "And it wasn't Sharlene." She leaned toward Alex. "Those were my I-wanna-forage-what-I-cook days. That didn't last long."

Sharlene and Jackie smiled at each other.

"Any updates?" Jackie asked. "Have you heard from Hank?"

Sharlene shook her head, her face shrouded in concern. "I assumed he was with you."

Jackie's voice caught in her throat. "He took on three martial arts assholes. Last I saw, they threw him through a window. They took me after that."

"Oh, dear," Sharlene said. "That's not good." She turned away and dabbed her eye. "Oh, dear." Sharlene walked behind the counter and rummaged through a drawer before pulling out a set of keys. "Let's get you both settled and see if we can find out anything about him."

They left the Crosstrek in the tourist information lot in case the car had been tracked. Sharlene mentioned another spirit tracker would take the vehicle. They hopped into Sharlene's Range Rover and drove toward Boynton Canyon. Tears welled in Alex's eyes as they passed more terracotta red rocks and dark-green pines set against the deep-blue sky. To her, there was nothing more beautiful.

She began remembering there was more to life than New York City. It had been an addiction, a real one. Alex never understood why she loved the city so much, with the dirt, crime, noise, and aggression everywhere. It wasn't healthy, but it had been the only place she'd wanted to be. The city was so big and diverse, Alex could walk out her door and reinvent herself anytime she wanted, whenever she wanted. When she lived there, New York was all that mattered, and leaving was impossible. Where does a person go after the center of the universe?

But here, among the terracotta red rocks and deep blue sky, Alex remembered there was more to life than the Big Apple. The city wasn't the center of the universe—New Yorkers told themselves that in order to survive the chaos. But New York City was an illusion, and Sedona was her detox.

Sharlene turned onto a private dirt road and drove up to a gate. After entering, they weaved to the back of the complex. Alex sensed eyes on her as they got out of the car, but saw no one.

She peered at the sprawling southwestern adobe-style mansion in front of her, then looked at Sharlene.

Sharlene smiled mischievously. "People loan us their houses for a certain amount of time," she said, her amber eyes twinkling. "And I see nothing wrong with finding the best."

Alex nodded and followed her inside. Floor-to-ceiling windows showcased the red rocks all around them. The enormous living room was open to the kitchen. They walked to the kitchen area, where Alex and Jackie settled at the large, exquisitely crafted wooden table.

Sharlene set two mugs and a porcelain teacup on the table and joined them. Without a word, she made clear the teacup was hers. She reached for the insulated carafe of hot water.

"Tea?" she asked, nodding toward a basket of tea bags.

"Uh," Alex said, glancing around the kitchen.

"Prefer coffee?" Jackie asked.

"Yes, please."

Jackie stood and started making a pot of coffee, then looked at the women. "What's going on, Sharlene? I'm out of touch with everything."

Sharlene brushed some crumbs off the table. "We discovered who's behind this." Once Jackie placed a cup of coffee in front of Alex, Sharlene continued. "Do you know who Jackson Wilson or JT is?"

"Of course," Jackie said.

Alex nodded as she put a generous amount of milk and sugar in her coffee. Everyone on the planet knew JT. Jackson Thomas Wilson was so rich and powerful, he only needed letters for a name. He owned the largest shipping company and retail store in the world, ShopMe. The global kingpin had tentacles everywhere. He was even in the ridiculous race to Mars with the other top billionaires.

Sharlene removed her tea bag and placed it on a saucer. She turned to Alex and Jackie. "Okay. Hold on to your mugs and let this sink in."

Alex tensed; she already knew she didn't want to hear what was coming.

"It seems JT's the person who's been extracting energy from the spirits. When he takes their energy, something goes wrong and they fall to earth and materialize as one of us. They lose their powers and memory. Like you've reported about Crystal."

"Shut the front door." Jackie pulled out her American Spirits and took a drag from an unlit cigarette. She picked up her tea and softly blew on it.

"Oh, come on," Alex said. JT was a successful businessman that most of the world looked up to. The blue skies and red rock beauty might have momentarily softened her, but Alex felt her anger and annoyance course through her veins again. Her eyes searched the room for a liquor cabinet.

Sharlene took Alex's hand. She tried to pull away, but Sharlene clamped on like a mother afraid of losing her child.

"No, honey, he *is* doing this." Sharlene gently squeezed her hand. "Don't worry; I know it's hard to believe."

Alex's hair streaked anger black and stress magenta as her face flushed. "Look, I've been through a lot these past few days." She pulled her hand away. "But this is going too far." She shook her head. "I don't believe in angels or spirits, let alone having energy sucked out of anything. And some billionaire's responsible? You sound like activists, blaming the rich person."

Sharlene nodded. "It's okay. You don't have to believe. We'd just like your help."

Alex crossed her arms. "I'm sorry, but I've got nothing. I can't help you."

Sharlene gave her a grandmotherly smile. "You're here, so you're part of this."

Alex ignored her comment. "Why would JT do this?"

Sharlene took a quick sip of tea and put her cup down. "He's conquered the world. What's left?"

"Other universes, it seems." Jackie pushed back her chair and headed to the freezer. She pulled out some ice cubes and wrapped them in a dish towel, then gently placed the cubes against her jaw.

Sharlene continued when Jackie rejoined them at the table. "I've heard the discovery was a mistake. His scientists were trying to do something else."

"What?" Jackie asked.

"We don't know." Sharlene leaned in. "We're not exactly sure what he's doing all this for. But he's certainly not trying to help the poor."

Alex looked at Sharlene and Jackie's serious faces nodding at her in unison. She screamed at herself on the inside. She wouldn't let it happen again. During her days in the music industry and her years with Finn, Alex had been open-minded, and even though she might have been naïve, she'd believed in possibility. She'd had hope. And she'd believed in her dreams.

But in a matter of months, she'd gone from five-star living in New York City to being homeless with some strangers in Sedona. An ugly bitterness coursed through her veins. She wouldn't let Sharlene and Jackie suck her into their delusions like others had in the past. She sighed and re-scanned the room for booze.

"Brace yourself. There's more." Sharlene leaned in. "We found out something's wrong with the spirits, and JT's doing tests on them. They start phasing in and out, and eventually they disappear. We don't know where to, though."

"Oh," accidentally fell out of Alex's mouth.

"What?" Jackie asked.

"Nothing," Alex replied.

"Sweetheart, what? Did you see something?"

Alex hesitated, then said, "I thought I saw Crystal fade a couple times while we were driving out here." She looked at the two women. "But I'm sure it was nothing. I was tired."

Sharlene and Jackie exchanged glances, their faces grave.

"This is ridiculous. I'm sure my eyes were playing tricks on me," Alex said.

"No." Sharlene shook her head. "I'm sure you saw it. And you've confirmed it's happening."

"Wait," Jackie said. "They could be going back where they came from."

Sharlene shook her head. "I wish that were true, but our team thinks JT's messing with the quantum field."

"Come on," Alex said.

Concern clouded Sharlene's face. "We've got some of the top scientists in the world helping us, Alex. They don't completely understand what's happening, but they're positive it's not good."

"Like end-of-the-world not good?" Jackie asked.

"There's a chance," Sharlene said. "That's why we need to find Crystal and figure out what's going on."

Alex closed her eyes tightly. They were insane.

Chapter Five

Something pinched Crystal's left arm.

"I think she's awake," a voice said through the haze that swirled through her head.

"Doesn't matter," said another male voice. "We're almost done."

Crystal faded into darkness. When she opened her eyes, she was back in her windowless cell on the cot. She had a hazy memory of getting exhausted after eating, then being wheeled into a lab or an operating room. She was sure they were drugging her food, but she had to eat. And she couldn't fight them. Whoever *they* were.

Grimacing, she put her hands to her head. Her skull was ready to crack open. "Ohhhhh." She rocked side to side on her steel cot, gently massaging her scalp. She found it hard to focus and see straight. Or think.

The keypad beeped and the lock to her cell clicked. If they were taking her in for more tests, she knew she would die. Which was ironic because she'd supposedly been dead already, but the pain was excruciating.

She shut her eyes and turned to the wall, pretending to be unconscious. Someone slipped into her room.

A paper cup touched her mouth. "Take this," a warm male voice said as two pills rolled onto her lips. She opened her mouth slightly and let them slide onto her tongue. A cold metal cup followed. Reflexively, Crystal swallowed the water and pills.

"I can't stay," the voice said. "I'm Zak, here to help. I'll be back."

Crystal opened her eyes. A man in his mid-twenties with soulful black eyes, brown skin, and waist-length black hair tied in a ponytail leaned over her.

Zak stepped back from her cot. "Don't take the pills they give you at night. They mess with your head."

The young man disappeared as quietly as he'd come. Crystal lay back and fell into a deep sleep.

Sometime later, when she opened her eyes, her migraine had vanished. Crystal felt rested, like after a deep night's sleep.

The days blurred together. Between the drugs, confinement, and tests, she might have been there for days or weeks. Someone was always wheeling her to be poked, prodded, and experimented on. Crystal was connected to wires, injected with unknown substances, and monitored for hours. But she was unconscious for the last set of experiments.

She woke with her usual grogginess as a tray of food appeared through the bottom of the door. Today was a round, brown blob of a meat-like substance, so it was evening and dinnertime. At least to Crystal.

Famished, she picked up the tray and put it on her lap. She ate the peas and potatoes but left the brown blob. As Crystal chewed some very hard bread, she stabbed the blob with her fork and picked it up. She turned it over and sniffed, gagging at the smell.

She looked at the gelatinous gravy and saw something white in the sauce. She took her plastic knife and poked at it. A piece of waxed paper covered in the brown glob slid into view.

Crystal bent in closer and turned it over. She scraped off the congealed gravy. Etched crudely into the plastic coating was "B Ready."

She glanced around her empty cell. "Be ready?" she said. "Be ready for what?" She wiped the last bits of gravy off the plastic paper and looked closely for clues. This might be part of the tests. Or perhaps something was going to happen.

Crystal stared at the message, her brain spinning, question after question popping into her mind. She had nothing to do to get ready, so she was prepared. Every few days, a new set of dark blue hospital scrubs appeared under the door, and the dirty ones were taken away. There was nothing to organize or pack. Her only personal items were her biker jacket and Converse sneakers. At least she'd been able to keep them. She always had them on, even when sleeping.

Expectantly, she sat on her bed, staring at the door. But nothing happened. Hours passed. She strained to hear the slightest sound. Her eyes grew heavy, and even though she did her best to stay awake, she nodded off.

When the keypad beeped, she bolted upright. The door clicked open. Crystal held her breath. It could be a guard, or it could be someone to harm her.

Zak, wearing all black, silently slid into the room, looking nervous but determined. He held his hand out to Crystal and whispered, "No time. I'll explain later." She took it and let him guide her out of the cell.

They ran down the hallway as quietly as possible. Still groggy from the drugs, Crystal moved hesitantly.

"You can do it. Just stay behind me," Zak said as they continued down identical-looking corridors.

They rounded a corner and headed down another hall. Two men in military fatigues stepped into the end of the corridor, blocking their way. They both held large guns in their hands.

"Shit," fell out of Zak's mouth. "Annihilators."

He grabbed Crystal and lunged for the closest door. After punching in his access code, he pushed her into the room. He entered more numbers into the keypad and joined her. Zak shut the door and leaned against it. "We can't get hit by those guns."

"Obviously," Crystal said.

"No, you don't understand. Someone at the lab said they're not normal guns. They not only kill, but they also annihilate you from existence. No rebirth, no afterlife, no continuing of your consciousness. You might not have my beliefs, but trust me, those things are bad. I don't know what they're called, but I call them annihilators."

"You mean...?"

Zak nodded. "Yes. It shouldn't be possible, but the energy that makes you up gets destroyed. You cease to exist. In any form, dimension, or reality. Forever." He glanced at the metal door. "And I worry they do more damage than that."

"Is that possible?"

Zak kept his back to the cell door. "Not sure, but we have to stay clear of them."

Crystal's eyes widened. Annihilation had never occurred to her. The idea of being wiped permanently from existence of any form shook something deep inside her. An odd sensation spread across her stomach and chest: fear.

"You need to do everything I say. Follow any move I make. No matter what." Zak looked into her eyes. "Understand?"

Crystal nodded, searching his eyes. He might be young in age, but she saw and felt the depth and wisdom of generations reflected in his gaze. The heavy feeling inside her chest lifted.

The pounding footsteps came closer.

Zak reached out and took her hand. "Trust me. The test you just had—something went wrong."

Crystal nodded.

"Kick the wall," Zak said.

"What?"

"Try to kick the wall."

Crystal lifted her foot and swung it at the wall.

"What the...?" she said as her foot sank into the concrete.

"I'll explain later. No time."

Crystal nodded.

The footsteps stopped. Beeps sounded and the handle jiggled, but the door remained shut. Angry fists pounded on the thick metal. More beeping, but the lock held firm. Zak must have jammed the system. The sound of bodies slamming against the door echoed throughout the room. Then silence.

Zak took her hand. "We have to get out. They'll probably blow it open."

Crystal grasped him firmly as he moved toward the wall. She tensed.

"Don't let go." Zak stopped inches from one side of the room and grabbed her wrist. He held her tightly and turned his body to the right.

Crystal stepped back with the movement, then headed directly toward the concrete. She closed her eyes and tensed as she prepared to make contact. A whooshing went through her as she hit the wall, not a sound but a sensation. When she opened her eyes, she saw blurry movement all around her.

Before she understood what was happening, they were out. Stars twinkled at them as they landed in the open desert.

"Run," Zak said. "We'll talk later."

They raced from the lab. There was enough moonlight to see outlines and silhouettes of the large rocks and cacti all around. Crystal ran carefully as she kept up with Zak. When they reached the fence surrounding the lab, Zak turned and grabbed her hand. They rushed straight through the metal barrier and ran until the terrain became rougher and large rocks were scattered across the landscape.

Crystal's eyes adjusted to the moonlight as they hopped and weaved across the terrain. Their pace slowed as the landscape became clogged with boulders blocking their way.

Zak stopped.

Crystal bent over to catch her breath. "What happened?"

"Later," he said softly. "We're still not safe."

She saw his silhouette stand at attention, his face tilted up to the night sky.

Crystal heard a sound in the distance.

They stood frozen to their spot, listening.

The sound came closer, boots crunching across the ground.

"Shit," Zak exclaimed quietly. He shoved Crystal between two boulders and pushed himself in after her. Cold rock pressed in on three sides, Zak next to her. She saw stars twinkling through the small gap behind him.

"I don't know if it's safe for us to melt into the rock and stay there," Zak whispered. "I worry we'll get stuck, so let's be still and hope they don't see us. We'll disappear if we have to."

Crystal nodded.

More rocks moved. A gruff voice said, "They're here somewhere. Keep searching."

"Nothing so far," another male replied.

Zak took her hand and held tight. She felt a guard feet from them. The sweep of a flashlight brushed by the small opening behind Zak. It probed through the darkness. She held her breath. She felt the light beam shine on them.

Crystal froze. She saw the silhouette of a man. She was blinded as he pointed the beam directly at Zak and her. He moved the light away from their eyes. He wore black military gear and rugged hiking boots. His thin turquoise-beaded necklace caught Crystal's eye. He stared directly at her and then at Zak. She saw them both nod almost imperceptibly to each other.

There was a suspended pause. Crystal held her breath as time stopped.

The man stepped back and turned. "Nothing, sir," he yelled to the other guard.

Heavy boots slowly walked away. Zak grabbed her tighter, silently telling her not to move.

Slowly, the crunching of stone faded away. An occasional shout rang out, but the sound grew more and more faint. Crystal continued to hold Zak, who let out a long sigh.

"He shined his flashlight right on us," Crystal said, relaxing her grip.

Zak stepped out from the boulders. "That was Kele. We worked together at the lab." He helped Crystal out from the rock. "I'm not the only one who thinks something bad is happening there." He smiled at her. "We might have more allies than we realize." He nodded slightly. "All that matters is we got away."

The two walked deeper into the desert.

***

After what seemed like hours of walking in silence, Crystal stopped. "What happened at the lab? We ran through a wall."

Zak paused and turned toward her. "Let's take a break."

They both sat on a large rock. Zak pulled out a canteen from his cargo pants. After they drank some water, he began. "About six months ago, I was hired to help with an amnesia study. Or that's what I was told. I was a lab assistant, but I also became a runner, so I often wheeled people to and from their tests." He took another swig of water. "I believed what I'd been told—that we were working on an amnesia study. I had no reason not to. Until the last subject came through." He smiled at Crystal. "I called her Angel."

He looked into the night sky. The moon shone over them like a beacon. "I overheard a doctor say she wasn't doing well. And they needed more tests performed right away. Invasive ones."

Crystal looked at the ground. "What's that mean, invasive?"

Zak bent over, picked up a couple of rocks, and rubbed them together as he looked at her. "They were talking about drilling into her brain."

Crystal's jaw dropped. "You can't be serious."

Zak nodded in the moonlit darkness, then turned to her. "That's why I helped you. They were doing the same to you tomorrow."

"Holy crap," Crystal said. She looked up and watched a shooting star spread its magic across the sky.

Zak followed her gaze. "The stars here are so amazing."

She nodded. "What happened to Angel?"

"Angel was called S42 on her paperwork because she didn't know her name." He smiled softly. "I named her Angel because she was the most amazing person I'd ever met."

Crystal smiled into the darkness. "So you two…?"

Zak threw the stones into the desert. "Oh, no, no. We barely knew each other." He looked down and sighed. "Though I wish we'd had time."

"I'm sorry."

"It's all right." He picked up a few more rocks and rolled them around in his hands.

"Wait," Crystal said. "S42. Does that mean she was the forty-second test subject? There were that many before me?"

"I've never thought about it," Zak said. "S25 was there when I started, so you might be right. You were S43. The lab must have assigned each person the next consecutive number." Slowly, he shook his head. "But they didn't stay long. A couple days or a week possibly." He glanced at Crystal. "You've been there longer than anyone else I've seen." He continued to slowly shake his head. "They would vanish."

A gasp escaped Crystal. "Do you mean...?"

"I don't know anything," Zak said. "Except that they disappeared. We were told they went to another facility, but I don't believe it."

They paused and looked at the dazzling night sky. The arm of the Milky Way stretched above them, billions of stars twinkling for the world to see. But so few looked up.

Zak looked at her, a serious expression coloring his face. "Angel told me she didn't remember anything before showing up in Montana a couple of weeks earlier. She made it to Missoula, where she was kidnapped and brought to the lab. Because everyone who came in had amnesia, we first thought they'd claimed kidnapping because of their condition. But Angel didn't believe what the lab folks were saying. She didn't know who she was but knew she had more than amnesia."

Crystal nodded. "Did she ever discover the truth?"

"I started snooping around for her but didn't find anything." Zak looked into the distance. "The night before we left, the lab techs freaked out. Something went wrong with an experiment. Angel survived, but they were concerned it damaged her. They'd planned on more tests the next day to figure out what happened. She told me that after she returned to her cell, she kicked the wall in frustration and put her foot through the concrete. She realized she could walk through a wall or a closed door if she used force, like by hitting or running at it."

"Why didn't she just escape through the wall?"

Zak sighed. "She was afraid she'd get stuck inside. And she didn't know the layout of the lab or grounds." He looked at his hands. "We'd already been planning to escape, so I'd like to think she wanted to go with me."

"What happened then?"

"I was completely shocked and didn't believe what she was saying, even after she shoved her arm through the wall to prove it. Who can do that? This might sound crazy, but she thought she was more than human. I didn't believe her.

"When I learned about the tests, I tried to sneak Angel out. I made the mistake of taking us through the front of the building. I thought I could sign her out like any patient who wanted to leave a study. We were told the subjects were there voluntarily and could leave anytime." Zak looked sadly at Crystal. "But they caught us at the front gate."

"I'm sorry."

He shook his head again. "I pushed her away and took on the guard, but in the scuffle she was shot with one of those guns you saw at the lab." He looked off into the distance. "And evaporated."

"Oh, my," slipped from Crystal's mouth.

"I also wasn't sure I'd go through the wall if I was holding her. And didn't realize we could run through the security fence like we did." Zak sighed. "If I'd known, maybe we would have tried a different way out."

"You weren't sure you'd go through with me?" Crystal asked.

Zak nodded. "That's why I threw you against the wall so hard. I thought at least you'd be free. The last test you had was the same experiment done on April that gave her the ability to run through walls."

Crystal nodded but remained silent.

Zak continued, "When I came to your cell, I'd been planning to take you out through the back exit. I had it timed so the guards would be away on their rounds. But when we got trapped, I didn't see another option except to throw you through the wall. And pray I'd go through with you."

"Thank you," Crystal said. "You could have gotten into so much trouble."

Zak looked out over the night desert. "There's a moment in our lives where we choose what we believe in. We can stand up for what's right or cower in fear. Angel was my deciding moment. After she died, I promised myself I'd never back down from trying to right a wrong." He gazed at the stars. "I've chosen to live on the side of light. No matter what." He looked back at Crystal. "I believe we create reality through our decisions."

Nodding, Crystal gently patted Zak's knee. "It's my turn now. I have some news for you, if you think you can handle it."

"Of course. No matter what."

"Okay," Crystal said with a slight smile. "Just prepare yourself." She took a deep breath and continued. "I'm a spirit, not human. Angel was one also, I'm sure. We were once human. But something's happened, and we've lost our powers and memory, and we materialized back on Earth."

"Wow" fell from Zak's mouth.

Crystal laughed. "It's so weird saying it out loud to someone."

He looked deep into her eyes as the moon reflected off his pupils. Zak didn't move for what seemed ages. Finally, he said, "I'm in shock and don't know what to say. But I believe you. It makes sense on some inner level. And it fits with who I believed Angel to be." He sat back. "Wow."

"I had the same reaction when I found out."

Zak stood and brushed the sandy dirt off his hands. "There's so much I want to ask, but it's still not safe. They might try to track us down with helicopters or four-by-fours, so let's keep going. We'll talk later."

They walked until lights appeared in the distance. As they got closer, Crystal noticed a campground.

Zak touched her arm lightly. "Be quiet and careful," he said as they got close.

They inched their way to the edge of the grounds, staying hidden behind the juniper trees now scattered across the landscape.

Zak put his finger to his mouth, signaling Crystal to be quiet. They turned back to the campground. Crystal saw some chairs at a fire pit, along with a few tents and camper vans.

She froze as a branch snapped, then turned and saw two men looking at them.

"Hello," the pasty one squeaked with a British accent. He waved his rubbery arm in the air as a greeting. "I'm Aaron." He pointed to his companion. "This is Nate."

Crystal stepped toward Zak and eyed both men. They were the oddest pair. The lanky, pasty one, Aaron, looked like an aging teenager with his pale, smooth complexion and gangly arms and legs. He wore a black T-shirt with "Foo Fighters" emblazoned on the front, ripped khaki shorts, and sandals. With white socks. The other wore green army fatigues and a black T-shirt several sizes too small for his hulky, muscular chest. His face was tanned and lined with creases from sun and stress. He looked like he'd single-handedly fought a war. And won.

"What do you want?" Zak asked, putting his arm protectively around Crystal.

Aaron grabbed his Gumby arm with his other hand and pulled it down. His eyes danced with childish joy. "We're camping here, and we wanted to say hi."

Crystal and Zak exchanged glances.

"You need to be careful," Aaron said. "Have you heard the news?"

They both shook their heads.

"Came on the shortwave. There's a search for a couple who escaped a top-security facility."

"Did they say who they were?" Zak asked.

"No, but they said they were dangerous," Aaron replied. "They might be murderers or something."

Crystal and Zak nodded but said nothing.

"A search party is also coming this way."

Zak hesitated. "Oh, um."

Aaron waved the two toward him. "Come back to my van. No questions asked."

Crystal and Zak looked at each other again, uncertainty written on their faces.

"We don't want to bother you," Crystal said.

Aaron giggled like a schoolkid. "You're no bother at all. We've got plenty of stuff. Happy to share."

Crystal hesitated. Her gut told her not to trust either of them, especially the pasty one. But if the search party was headed toward them, they needed to do something quick. And the silent one looked like he could protect anything.

She turned to Zak. "I don't know," she told him.

"Oh, enough of this," squeaked Aaron.

Zak and Crystal turned back. Nate stood in front of them with a gun pointed at Zak's face.

"I'll try again," Aaron said cheerfully. "Let's go back to the camper." Nate glared at them both.

"Oh," Aaron continued in his gleeful, childlike voice. "Try to run and Nate will kill you." He leaned in toward the two and stage whispered, "There's a silencer on the gun."

Aaron half skipped to the van as Crystal and Zak followed. Nate brought up the rear, gun still drawn. There was nowhere to run, and Crystal could tell Nate wasn't fooling around.

They all piled into the camper.

Crystal stepped inside, a look of surprise spreading across her face. Aaron nearly jumped for joy when he saw her expression. "Great, isn't it? I just got it. Great way to travel." He bounced over to the kitchen area. "Look. It's a mini kitchen with a small induction stove and refrigerator." He opened the fridge. "Drink?" He pulled out four bottles of water.

Crystal nodded, more from shock than saying yes.

"Sit." He pointed to the table and benches Nate had pulled down from the van wall. All while keeping the gun on them.

Crystal and Zak sat across from each other as Aaron placed the bottles on the table.

"Through?" Zak mouthed to her as he glanced at the side of the van.

Crystal nodded slightly. She grabbed Zak's wrists tightly and threw herself at the side of the camper. She hit the steel with a thud and dropped back into her seat.

Aaron laughed. "Oh, that's a sturdy wall, that is."

Crystal tried again and fell back into her seat.

"Whatever you're doing, stop," Nate barked, his gun now trained at Crystal's temple.

Crystal kicked the side of the van and stubbed her toe. "Ow," she said.

Zak looked at her and subtly shook his head.

"Give me your shoes," Nate barked, keeping the gun aimed at them.

"What?" Crystal asked.

Nate stepped toward Crystal. "Take off your shoes." He raised the gun to Crystal's face. "Now."

Zak reached under the table and began to untie his laces.

"Oh." Crystal kicked off her sneakers and held them out to Nate.

The bodyguard grabbed both pairs and tossed them to Aaron, who raised his arms and batted them away from his face. The gawky stranger picked up the shoes and moved to a door. "And look," he said as he opened it. He pointed inside. "Toilet and shower. And back there," he said, gesturing to the back of the van, "A queen-size bed." Aaron disappeared into the bathroom with the shoes. He reappeared without them and giggled as he sat next to Crystal. "It's so perfect."

Aaron didn't seem to notice the gun being pointed at her and Zak. He opened his bottle of water and took a long drink.

"You don't have any gum, by any chance, do you?" Crystal asked. She looked at Zak sheepishly. She'd chewed her last piece the day before.

"Not sure," Aaron replied. "But I've blown some bubbles in my time." He giggled. He rose and rummaged through the pantry compartment full of cookies, candy, and other assorted junk food.

"Well, I'll be damned," Aaron said. He pulled out a baggie full of Bazooka gum.

"Thanks," Crystal said as she took it. She popped one of the pink pieces into her mouth and pocketed the rest.

Footsteps crunched outside the camper. Nate stood up and put his finger to his mouth, telling them to be quiet. He pointed the gun at Crystal and Zak, motioning for them to move to the back. He followed and opened a drawer under the bed and gestured for them to get in.

They hesitated. Nate pointed the gun at Crystal's head. "Get in," he hissed as he pointed to the open storage space.

"Just do it," Zak whispered to her. Silently, Crystal stepped into the storage space under the bed, then pressed herself against the side of the compartment as Zak squeezed in next to her.

Nate tossed in their water and shoes and quickly shut the drawer. A soft thud above them meant someone had taken a seat on the bed. Judging by the lightness of the sound, it was Aaron.

Crystal wrapped her arms tightly around Zak's chest and stomach. "What happened with the wall?" she whispered in his ear.

Zak turned his head toward her. "No idea, but maybe your powers were temporary."

Crystal nodded as her heart pounded in her ears. She jumped when she heard a hard knock on the driver's-side door.

She leaned into Zak. From her soul to her shoes, she was exhausted. She quietly chewed her gum, sucking out as much sugar as possible.

Gruff, muffled voices came from outside the van.

"There's no one here," Aaron said in a high-pitched voice. "Take a look."

"There's nowhere to go in here," Nate added.

"Should we surrender and go with those guys?" Crystal whispered.

Zak shook his head. "I think it's harder to get out of the lab than this van."

"But the gun."

"Remember that gun at the lab? That's way worse."

"Oh. Right."

They heard more muffled sounds. Nate must have blocked the search party from leaning in too far.

"We'll tell you if we see anyone wandering around," Aaron said. "I hope they're not dangerous or anything."

The door closed, and Nate's footsteps headed back toward them.

"Something's wrong," Nate said, his voice stopping at the bed. "It's not normal for a search team not to search a place. They must know they're here."

"How in the world is that possible?" Aaron asked. "We let them look inside and there was nothing."

"You hired me to protect you, right?" There was a slight pause as Aaron probably nodded. "Well, I'm telling you something's off. They'd be stupid not to have thermal-imaging devices."

"They what?"

Crystal heard Nate sigh. "Meaning they can read heat signatures."

"Oh," squeaked out of Aaron.

"Yeah. Instead of seeing two heat signatures, you and me, they're going to see four."

"Maybe they didn't bring the equipment."

Crystal heard the banging sounds of Nate quickly packing the camper. "I've done this work for over twenty years. They'd never search for anything without a thermal-imaging device. You might be good at your job, but this is my area of expertise."

The sound of Aaron's bouncing leg filled the van. "We should go then?"

"Yes, immediately. I'm sure they're reporting in, and then they'll ambush us. We only have minutes to get away."

"We have to escape," Zak told Crystal.

The drawer was roughly pulled open. Aaron turned and raced to the front passenger side of the camper. As Crystal and Zak climbed out, Nate thrust his gun in Aaron's hand and jumped into the front seat.

Zak reached back in the drawer and gave Crystal her sneakers. "Get them on. We have to jump."

Crystal nodded and slipped on her shoes as Zak laced up his boots.

"Keep the gun on them," Nate said to Aaron as he started the van and raced out of the campsite.

Chapter Six

JT slashed his lightsaber through the air and screamed into his speakerphone. "What do you mean, she got away? I own everything: cell towers, tracking devices, satellites that can take pictures of a license plate. How the hell did they get away?"

"No idea, sir," came through the phone. "We had her cornered in a cell, but she and her accomplice got away. It's like they went through the wall."

"Well, find them, you morons," JT yelled. "I don't care what you do. I need that woman, and I need her *now*."

The test subject at the lab had survived longer than any of the others. JT's super-secret research team had told him she might be the key to figuring out their extraction issues—and other potentially catastrophic side effects his procedures might be causing. They couldn't lose her.

The global kingpin let out an ear-piercing scream and a nose-destroying, acidic wind explosion. He stormed across his black stone floor, slashing and swishing his way through the imaginary rebel alliance of his enemies.

He punched the intercom button on his conference table. "Get in here *now!*"

His office door flew open. "Yes, sir," said Four of Five, recoiling from the stench.

JT kicked his ten-foot fake ficus tree with a vengeance before looking at the stranger in his office. "Who the hell are you?"

The assistant visibly shook. "I'm Ben, sir."

"Ben? Who the fuck is Ben? What's your number?"

The shaking continued. "I'm Four of Five, sir."

JT put down his sword. "I don't know you. Where's One, Two, and Three?"

"Getting your dry cleaning, following your ex-wife, and returning that painting you hated to the gallery."

"They should be back," JT screamed.

"You sent them less than five minutes ago, sir. I can help with anything. Just let me know what you need."

"Don't you *dare* talk to me that way," JT screamed. He swung his lightsaber into the tree, breaking the sword in two. He dropped the broken half he was holding. His face turned deep red as a wet wind expulsion rocketed out of his ass. JT picked up a heavy crystal award on the shelf next to him and hurled it at the assistant. The crystal globe left a dent in the door where Four's head had been a second earlier.

JT screamed toward the outer office, "Get whoever's responsible for this online *now*. Audio on his end."

The global kingpin held one-way video calls where he saw the person he was speaking to, but they only heard his voice booming throughout the room they were in.

"Yes, sir," yelled Four of Five from the safety of the other room.

"And what the fuck is a fake tree doing in my office? Get it out *now*."

"Yes, sir," floated back in a shaky monotone.

Ignoring his wet whities, JT ran his short fingers through his somewhat-real dark hair. His insulated briefs could hold the mess before he needed a change.

He stormed back to his desk, where he picked up his processed protein drink and threw it at the window. No one should get away from him. He was one of the most powerful men in the world, with the most sophisticated tracking devices, and had tens of thousands of people working for him.

Toot-toot-toots of frustration shot out his ass, staining his briefs even more. Squeezing his cheeks, he hobbled over to his television monitor.

JT's intercom buzzed. Four of Five's voice came through the speaker. "Dr. Maximilian Underhill. He only has audio." Four clicked off before JT could respond.

JT emptied his stormtrooper dispenser full of high-potency antacids into his mouth and found his remote. He clicked on his seventy-two-inch combo TV/computer monitor.

A sweaty, disheveled man with fear slathered over his face appeared on the screen. His white hair looked glued at the base but stuck up and bounced around on the ends, like an atomic mushroom cloud. His white lab coat was askew and stained with an assortment of greasy takeout meals. He fidgeted nervously in his seat and loudly blew his bulbous nose into a handkerchief.

JT walked to the screen, crunching loudly. "Who are you and what the fuck have you done?"

Dr. Max jumped, dropping his hankie. "Um, Dr. Maximillian Underhill. I run the lab..."

"I know what you do," JT said gruffly. "What the fuck did you do to lose your test subject? She was part of the experiment I needed done."

Dr. Max shifted uncomfortably in his chair, his eyes searching the ceiling and walls. He wiped sweat off his forehead with his sleeve. "Your Seattle office sent me new parameters for the research. We did exactly what your people instructed, but somehow the subject escaped with one of my employees."

JT fought back the urge to punch the six-foot-wide television monitor. He turned to kick a plastic tree but saw them both silently bobbing out of his office, Four and Five of Five barely visible through the leaves.

He turned back to the screen, his stomach boiling in protest. "Don't blame this on my office."

Dr. Max's fingers were stuck in his unkempt hair. He struggled to free them from his white steel-wool head. A bead of sweat rolled down the side of his face. "I'm sorry, sir. I wasn't implying that."

JT's fists and ass clenched. "I don't want apologies. How did they escape?"

Dr. Max shook his head, his fingers still stuck in his gelled hair. "We're not sure. Security was chasing them and had them cornered, but they got away. It was like they disappeared into thin air or ran through the wall."

A super-wet one was boiling up, an explosion even JT's insulated underpants wouldn't be able to contain.

"Security was everywhere," Dr. Max said. He yelped as he yanked his hand free. "We had everyone at the lab, from security to office cleaners, chasing after them. But every time someone got close, they disappeared." He sighed. "We simply aren't sure how they got out."

JT stomped his foot. "Stupidity, that's what it is. Fire all the security. Get a new team. And get twice as many. By *tomorrow*. If anyone else escapes or anything else happens, you're out of a job. Or worse."

Even though he knew Dr. Max couldn't see him, JT leaned in close to the screen. "I'll make sure you never get a job anywhere ever again. Are we clear?"

JT cut off the feed before Dr. Max could react. *Idiots*, he thought as he ran into his executive bathroom. He pulled down his almost-jeans and squatted over the toilet. An ass explosion of nuclear force erupted into the bowl; he'd made it just in time. JT was relieved as he sat on the heated seat and was sprayed with scented water and air dried. He kicked off his soiled whities and reached into his emergency drawer for a clean pair. To be safe, he also grabbed a fresh pair of black pull-on cotton with mock fly almost-jeans.

Dr. Max Underhill was JT's fifth lab director in a year, and he needed to keep him there. At least for now. He'd been the best of them all. Few people had the expertise JT needed and would hold to their nondisclosure agreement. He also wanted clueless men who believed the work was a study on curing amnesia and not experimenting on once-human entities.

The global kingpin rose from his throne, accidentally glancing in the mirror as he adjusted his pants. Before him the sad, lonely, pudgy face of his father looked back. JT recoiled from the realization. He had turned into *him*.

"*No!*" he screamed to the image he could not be.

Quickly, JT turned away and hit the intercom button by his toilet. "Get the mirrors out of here *immediately*." He turned his back to the reflection of who he really was. "There's no fucking way I'm that asshole," he mumbled.

The kingpin pushed down a growing emptiness and headed back into his office, cleaned, dried, and smelling pretty. Dr. Max's words sank in. He'd said it was like they disappeared or walked through walls. The security force had said the same thing. What if they actually had? The thing might have gotten back some of her abilities, which could be an enormous problem.

JT sat back at his desk. *Or it could be a massive boon*, he thought. It could be new technology he could sell. Defense departments worldwide would pay trillions for the technology to walk through walls. JT needed that spirit back immediately. He would show his father.

He pressed the intercom button. "Get intel on the thing that got away. All of it." He paused, then added, "Make sure One has it together by tomorrow." He clicked off before anyone could answer.

JT picked up his cell phone and opened his digital assistant. "Sam McMahon at The Society," he said to the machine. He sat back on his toasty, dry ass, putting his feet up. He could make much more than money from these beings. With help from The Society, the world and everyone on it would be his. JT laughed his evil villain laugh, the one he'd practiced since fourth grade when the boarding school bullying had started. The world would be his, all of it, so he might as well capture the heavens as well.

"McMahon," he said into his secure private phone. "Have I got an idea for you."

***

The silence was as loud as the screaming. Dr. Max looked at the blank wall in the windowless, empty room, his hands still shaking. Something was wrong. Something was definitely wrong. Why would anyone care so much about one study participant? They had a steady stream coming through. Each week or two, someone arrived.

Dr. Max returned to his office. No job was worth the amount of stress he was under. And being screamed at like that? No one had the right to yell like that. Even funders should have some manners. At sixty-five, Max was entitled to a little respect. He'd had enough.

The recent complaints came flooding back. Over the past three months, four of his researchers had quit. In their exit interview, each had stated they were being lied to. They believed something illegal and nefarious was going on because they couldn't analyze or look at full test results, only their piece of the work. Human resources also had informed the scientist that a growing number of support staff were quitting and claiming in their exit interviews that something unethical or illegal was occurring.

Dr. Max had laughed off the reports, believing the employees were unhappy because they weren't getting credit for their work. They were earning nearly double what they would get anywhere else. He had justified their leaving, convincing himself it was their ego talking. And support staff weren't paid well or given perks, so they were easily replaceable. Their average work expectancy was a year or two.

The scientist had to admit he'd brushed aside all the comments because he didn't want the hassle of dealing with other people's problems. He realized they were right: something was wrong.

Suddenly, Dr. Max didn't feel safe; the funder probably had people monitoring and spying on him. Had he been that blind?

Although he couldn't change the past, he could do something now. The scientist quickly logged into the accounts of each of his research assistants and fellow scientists. He knew he could get fired for breaking his contract, but he'd made his decision: he wasn't coming back. He copied all their data and results onto a thumb drive.

He rummaged around the back of his lightsaber storage cabinet until he found the info sheet he'd created for Sandra Carl, the secret temporary researcher assigned to his lab a few months earlier. He didn't trust her mysteriously appearing at the office and being so secretive, so he'd made a point of copying her logins and private information when she first started.

He broke into her account and downloaded everything he could find. Dr. Max then gathered his papers and laptop and left the building. His heart pounded furiously as he forced himself to walk at a normal pace. He was hyperventilating as he jumped into his Prius. He was definitely not James Bond.

Dr. Max left the research facility as fast as he could without looking obvious and headed for his house. The billowing white clouds and vast expanse of the deep-blue New Mexico sky stretched before him. He swerved as a tumbleweed bounced and rolled in front of the car. A week earlier, one had caused the automatic braking system to screech his new Prius to a halt in the middle of the highway.

The scientist relaxed back into his drive. And now there was Zak. His lab tech had run out on him without even a goodbye. He'd considered Zak a friend, even though he could have been his father. Max cringed; he could have been his grandfather.

He shook his head. He was getting old. Hair gel and new clothes might not be enough to find a partner. Or even close friends. All he knew was work.

Dr. Max smacked the steering wheel. Zak also tried to tell him something was wrong at the lab, but he had brushed the young man aside like the others.

The scientist steered clear of a few more tumbleweeds. What did Zak tell him? He couldn't remember. He'd been too busy ignoring complaints from everyone, so he hadn't listened. And he'd brushed aside the report about Zak trying to leave with a subject. Young people do young people things.

As Dr. Max pulled into his driveway, the obvious hit him. Zak had tried twice to leave with a test subject, and he'd succeeded the second time. He'd risked his job, even after being reprimanded, so it had to be more than youthful hormones.

Another realization struck him as he headed to the front door of his modest adobe home. Armed security had always been at the lab, but they protected the top-secret research. Could they also have been there to keep the test subjects prisoner?

When Dr. Max entered his house, his two best friends, long-haired red chihuahuas Fred and George, greeted him. They wagged their tails and rolled over for belly rubs. He gave them a quick hello and pet, then rushed into his office.

Normally, he never saw study participants until they were sedated and in the lab. Crystal was one of the first he'd spoken to before the test. And she'd asked him why she'd been kidnapped. Dr. Max hit his forehead with his hand. How could he have been so careless? And blind?

He'd ignored what Crystal was asking because of his rush to get the tests started. He was always behind schedule, so he even disregarded the test subjects to focus on his work and getting results.

Dr. Max sat at his desk and pulled out his private laptop and papers. He called Fred and George over and picked them up. Happily, they curled on top of each other in his lap, trying to plant kisses on his arms and neck.

He booted up his personal computer, the one not connected to the internet. The scientist was determined to uncover the truth about the research at the lab. As part of Dr. Max's employment contract, he was required to send all data he and his colleagues collected to another group in another location. His team wasn't permitted to analyze any of their results, so he never fully understood what they were working on, and he never saw results from their experiments.

He inserted the thumb drive he'd taken from the office and uploaded the information. Dr. Max had been told the funder wanted the research separated, so there would be less chance of bias. With all the funding he was given, along with his salary, the scientist had agreed without a second thought. Funders were often eccentric.

He stayed offline and only worked from his hard drive. He didn't want anyone virtually logging into his account and finding out what he was doing. Hours passed as he combed through mountains of data. At some point, Fred and George disappeared to their bed next to his desk.

Most of the team were looking at brain-wave energy, which wasn't surprising. But they'd also been looking at electromagnetic and infrared energy, auric fields, and something he wasn't completely sure he was looking at.

Auric fields were an uncommon subject for traditional scientists to study, but it was still energy. Dr. Max wasn't alarmed they were looking into alternative modalities, but the new data confused him. It was the work the temporary researcher Sandra Carl had conducted. Sandra was from the super-secret office in Seattle that was analyzing all the data his teams were generating. Any time the scientist asked her to clarify their work, she reminded him she had strict instructions not to share information with anyone.

Dr. Max found all the data from her tests and combed through the results. He gasped again. Although he wasn't an expert in the field, it seemed they were also looking at quantum energy output from the test subjects.

He scoured through the research and math. He wasn't a quantum physicist, but by the notes and journal entries attached to the research, along with the results and calculations, it appeared Sandra was looking at quantum entanglement and other aspects of quantum physics.

"Why?" Dr. Max mumbled as he booted up his connected laptop and opened an incognito window. The scientist searched through scientific databases to get up to speed on the subject, losing hours as he read piece after piece.

He woke with his face on the desk. Fred and George snored happily in their beds by his feet. Dr. Max grunted and sat upright, a piece of paper stuck to his hair. He pulled it off his head and saw the phrase "quantum entanglement" circled on the page. The scientist rubbed his eyes and looked back at his computer screen.

If two electrons could have simultaneous reactions, even light-years apart, Sandra might have found entanglement in objects larger than subatomic particles.

"No way," Dr. Max exclaimed. "No freaking way."

Fred and George stirred and looked up.

Dr. Max looked down at them and pointed to his screen. "Guys, I could be wrong, but I know I'm not. The funder's researching quantum energy in humans. Or…"

He turned back to his computer screen, pulled up the report he'd run earlier, and double-checked his results. He then triple-checked them.

"I don't understand," he said, reviewing his work again. Fred and George wagged their tails and gazed at him expectantly. Fred rolled over to show his belly.

Dr. Max smiled. "No, you two. You've had enough treats. And use the wee pads if you have to go." He looked back at his results. "It just can't be," he said, as he read and reread, then re-reread his work.

"Fred, George, you won't believe this."

The two dogs wagged their way over to Dr. Max's legs and looked up at him.

The scientist glanced down. "I know I'm not wrong, but I can't believe what I'm seeing." He pointed to his screen. "We're researching humans, energy from alternate dimensions, and quantum entanglement. I think—"

Dr. Max went back into Sandra's online folder and dug through her files. Buried in a folder within a folder within a folder was a document named "Ender." He clicked into it.

He gasped as he read Sandra's report. "This can't be true."

Dr. Max read the document again and shook his head. There, in black-and-white, were Sandra's notes. She matter-of-factly started by stating that her team in Seattle was interrupting quantum connections and disentangling spirit guides from humans in order to extract their energy.

She noted that she'd meticulously gone through all the research from the scientist's lab, but his group hadn't discovered anything that would allow her unit to locate specific celestial beings. For the foreseeable future, the energy extractors would continue to randomly target sections of quantum space in the hopes a spirit was caught in the beam.

The report also stated that Dr. Max's team had been unsuccessful in developing tests that could explain why the spirits had fallen to Earth as humans once they were disentangled. And the lab hadn't been able to stop the beings from disappearing within a few weeks of the separation. Because they were vanishing, secret researcher Sandra Carl concluded that how to target the spirits was currently more important than understanding why they were showing up.

Sandra continued with a theory: she believed humans and guides were inextricably linked and couldn't survive without the other. The researcher hypothesized the spirits were folding in on themselves and possibly disappearing into a new type of miniature black hole they were creating. She cautioned that if too many quantum collapses like that happened, in time it could create a larger black hole that could absorb the entire planet. She stated the issue needed to be the lab's top priority.

Sandra also cautioned that if spirits were disappearing within weeks or a couple months of the extraction procedure, the humans who were disconnected might also find themselves facing a similar fate, meaning the humans connected to the spirits JT was extracting might also die because of the disconnection. Sandra didn't know the how or why but believed it was a possibility.

The report concluded with her assertion that the timeframe was uncertain, but the funder's actions would eventually cause space-time to collapse in on itself, thus destroying the Earth and, in time, everything in the universe.

After staring in shock at his computer screen for at least ten minutes, Dr. Max jumped up. He looked at his dogs, his eyes wide-open. "Fred. George. We have to get out of here. *Now*."

The scientist raced around his house, packing for himself and his four-legged best friends. He realized his home was probably bugged, and someone could be watching his every move. He froze. If he was being watched, he was being obvious. *James Bond*, he thought to himself. *Be James Bond*. He slowed himself down.

"Yes," he told Fred and George, his voice rising in pitch as he tried to act like nothing was wrong. "You both deserve a holiday, don't you? Yes, you're both so cute. Let's take a road trip. What do you think about Ruidoso?"

George gave a short bark.

"Good," Dr. Max said a little too loud, gathering toys and blankets for the dogs. "We need a vacation. We've been working too hard."

He loaded his Prius as fast as he slowly could and sped in the other direction, away from the small town of Ruidoso. Once on Interstate 10, he turned to his chihuahuas. "What are we going to do, guys?"

Fred let out a short bark, his tail thumping.

"You're right!" Dr. Max exclaimed as he awkwardly searched his pockets and the front seat for his phone. "I'll text Zak. He might have some suggestions."

Chapter Seven

Crystal and Zak sat on the camper floor, gripping the side of the bed. They bounced up and down as Aaron shakily kept the gun trained in their direction.

"My neck hurts," the tech genius said with a whine as he turned toward Nate. "Do I have to keep pointing this thing at them?"

"Jesus Christ," Nate said, pushing away the gun now pointed at him. "That's not a toy. Keep it on them."

"But my neck."

"You're gonna have much less than a neck if you don't keep that gun on them."

Zak leaned into Crystal's ear. "Do you think we should—"

Before he could finish, their world turned upside down. Literally. Everything went into slow motion. The deafening sound, the screeching tires, the smell of rubber. Crystal and Zak were thrown across the camper. Crystal saw herself reach for Zak as metal screeched against metal.

A forceful thud spun the camper at an awkward angle. Crystal heard gunfire. It was like a dream.

Another crash tilted the van. Crystal and Zak slowly flew through the air—his long, black, silky hair flowing gracefully out behind him. The camper flipped on its side. They came down hard against the cupboards and refrigerator. Crystal landed with a violent jolt. She struggled to breathe as she looked around her; Zak wasn't moving.

The back door opened. A helmeted, masked figure jumped in over the bed and leaned over Crystal. "Can you move?"

She wasn't sure where she was.

"Crystal!"

She jumped at the sound of her name, then looked up.

"Are you okay?"

Crystal scanned her body and wiggled her fingers and toes. She turned her head from side to side. "I think so."

"Give me your hand."

The stranger lifted her and helped her out the door. As she touched the ground, she glanced back inside. Aaron was dangling sideways, his head and light brown curls bobbing in the air. His seat belt held him in place as his hands waved above his head. Loud squeaks came from his mouth. Someone must be holding him and Nate at gunpoint.

A sharp wind hit Crystal's face, bringing her back into her body. "Zak..."

"I got him." Another masked figure leapt into the camper opening, then bent over Zak, checking his pulse.

Crystal was whisked from the camper to what looked like a tank. As she got close, she saw it was a heavily armored SUV with a battering ram attached to the front.

She was too weak to think, let alone fight. The lab kidnappers had found her.

She was seated in the back. The masked figure carried Zak and placed him on the seat beside her. He joined them in the backseat.

Gunfire filled Crystal's ears as the stranger put his hand behind her head.

"Get down as far as you can."

She bent over; Zak was still unconscious.

The driver and front passenger jumped into the vehicle, guns still drawn. The passenger shot more rounds out the window as the SUV tank sped away.

Crystal looked out the back window. The camper van was crushed and on its side, flames flaring out the windows.

The front passenger turned to the backseat. "Hi, Crystal."

He took off his helmet and goggles, his ice-blue eyes crinkling as he smiled at her.

"Hank?" Crystal asked incredulously. His scruffy face had now sprouted a beard.

Hank laughed and put on his formfitting wraparound sunglasses. "Bet you didn't see that coming."

"I'm so happy to see you." She looked at Zak. "Is he going…?"

The soldier next to Crystal said, "He'll be okay. A concussion maybe, but don't worry. I'll check him again as soon as we can slow down."

Crystal turned back to Hank in disbelief. "What are you doing here?"

He laughed. "Helping you escape."

"But—"

"I've been tracking you since you were abducted, but the lab was a fortress, and I couldn't get in."

"I thought you were dead."

Hank grinned. "Takes more than a window and three assholes to put me down."

Crystal looked at him with admiration. He was relentless and so nonchalant about putting his life on the line for other people.

The SUV bounced over a pothole on the rutted dirt road. Hank put his hand on the roof of the car. "I was monitoring the facility. I saw the commotion and figured you'd escaped, but I couldn't find you." He put his arm down. "So I followed security from the lab. Put them out of their misery and here we are."

"You didn't..."

Hank snorted. "As much as I wanted to eliminate them, they're all alive. Battered and bruised, but alive."

Crystal felt the rumble and heard the explosion. She jumped and looked out the back window. Flames and black smoke reached up to the night sky. The acrid smell of burning fuel and rubber drifted into her nose.

"Well, no one will chase you now." Hank turned back to the front. "Let's get you to Sedona."

***

Sharlene, Jackie, and Alex sat at the kitchen table, the headquarters' unofficially official meeting place. Alex sipped her coffee while the other two drank tea and munched on the granola Sharlene had made that morning. After a couple weeks in Sedona, Alex wanted to get back to New Jersey. And a drink. Even though she loved the scenery and red rocks, the town brought back too many memories she wanted to forget. And there was no liquor in the house. She'd only managed to purchase alcohol a few times when she could sneak out. Someone always seemed to be around her, making her wonder if she was being monitored.

They all jumped at the sound of the front door opening. Sharlene rushed into the hallway.

Jackie stood to follow. She stopped as Sharlene came around the corner, smiling from ear to ear.

A squeal rang through the room. "Hank!" Jackie rushed over and wrapped her arms around her friend. "I was afraid we'd lost you."

Hank returned Jackie's hug, then held her at arm's length. "Come on, that was a minor scuffle."

Jackie smiled and gave him one more squeeze, then let go.

Behind Hank were Crystal and a young Native American man. Alex stood, relief washing over her. She surprised herself by caring.

"Crystal." Alex awkwardly semi-embraced Crystal before stepping back and giving her a once-over. "You're okay."

Crystal nodded and turned to Zak.

"Alex, this is Zak. He helped me escape." Crystal turned to him. "And Zak, this is Alex. She helped me when this nightmare started."

Alex and Zak shook hands. A tingle raced up Alex's arm as she blushed. Streaks of purple sprinkled her hair. *No!* her insides screamed.

The three joined the others at the kitchen table. Sharlene put out more mugs. She turned to Zak. "Tea or coffee?"

"Coffee if you have."

Sharlene poured him some from the thermos on the table.

"Thanks," Zak said, reaching for the mug.

"Well, thank goodness everyone's safe," Sharlene said after introductions and hellos were over. She turned to the new arrivals. "What happened?"

Crystal glanced at Zak, then at the table. "Zak might know more, but after they kidnapped me, I ended up in some kind of research facility or lab in southern New Mexico."

"I think it might be part of the Spaceport," Zak said. "It's in that area."

"They drugged me and were doing experiments," Crystal continued.

"Why?" Alex asked.

Crystal popped a fresh piece of Bazooka into her mouth and turned to Zak. "Can you explain?"

Zak nodded. "I did odd jobs and errands at the lab and got friendly with the head of the place. He often let me watch the experiments."

Crystal blew a bubble and sucked it back into her mouth with a loud crack.

"Crystal was in an exam room on the table when I first saw her," Zak said.

"What were they doing?" asked Sharlene.

"I'm not sure. They attached electrodes all over her head, and they were injecting her with different things. I guessed they were running experiments to look at brain-wave activity. Or something like that. They were trying to find a certain pattern or signature." Zak paused. "When we were hired, we were told we'd be working to cure amnesia, so at first no one questioned anything." He looked at Crystal. "After we escaped, Crystal explained who she is, so I'm sure something bad, and probably illegal, is going on there. I just don't know what."

Sharlene leaned in toward Zak. "This is very important. Did you ever see the test results?"

"No. They were all fed into a computer, and I never had access to the scientists' private accounts. I was more the errand boy."

Sharlene sat back. "We need to see those results."

"I'll go back," Hank replied. "I've cased the lab."

Sharlene shook her head. "Breaking into the lab isn't a good idea. You said it's a fortress."

Hank nodded. "It is."

"Sharlene," Alex said, "while you sort this out, do you mind if I go out and get some coffee?" She looked at her mug. "This stuff is pretty bad, and we just ran out." She looked at Zak. "Don't you think so?"

Zak smiled politely. "Well, let's just say it's not my cup of tea."

Jackie laughed. "Is Sharlene making the coffee again?" She stage-whispered to Zak, "She doesn't know how. And it usually tastes like mud."

"Do you mind?" Alex asked again.

"Of course not, dear." Sharlene picked up her wallet from the counter and held out a handful of twenties. "Go up to the light. There's a bakery there with delicious coffee and pastries." She pushed back her chair. "I wouldn't mind something myself. Can you get a few things for everyone?"

"Sure." Alex took the money and shoved it into her pocket. "Just anything?"

"Croissants and bakery goods, and anything else you want." Sharlene sat back and pointed toward Zak. "And take Zak with you, if he doesn't mind. I think we should stay in pairs."

Alex blushed through the butterflies that had settled into her gut. "Okay," she said to no one in particular, suddenly self-conscious. She hoped no one could translate the purple in her hair.

"Shouldn't he stay here while we talk?" Hank asked.

Sharlene shook her head. "He told us what he knows. We can figure out next steps while they're out."

"Great," Zak said, standing.

Alex jumped up. Somewhere in Sedona, a bottle of vodka had her name on it.

***

Alex and Zak hopped into Sharlene's Range Rover and headed up Boynton Pass Road. Towering red rock formations stretched in front of and around them.

"I forgot how beautiful this place is," she said as they curved past the entrance to the Devil's Bridge hike. "Until I came back. It's funny how you can love and hate something at the same time."

Zak turned to her. "You've been here before?"

Alex nodded as she concentrated on the road. "I lived here for a few years." She paused, then added, "Another lifetime ago."

She remembered the hikes, the sunsets, the peace of the land. And also the arguments with Skeater, the betrayals, the lying. She'd been so in love. And so blind. Why was he such an asshole?

"Lucky you," Zak said. "I hear there were fewer people back then."

She nodded. "By the look of the traffic, it's way more crowded now. But still gorgeous."

Zak nodded.

"After we get coffee, do you mind going to a supermarket, so I can get wine or something? I'm dying for a drink."

"Sure," Zak said.

They found the bakery and bought coffee and enough pastries for a few days. Zak left with enough freshly ground coffee beans for the two of them.

As he opened the passenger door, he froze. "Oh, shit. Get in. Quick."

They both jumped into the car. Zak ducked his head as far under the dashboard as possible.

"What in the world?" Alex started.

"Are those two guys still there? One has a red baseball cap."

Alex looked out the window. "Um, yeah. They're headed toward the bakery."

"Take some pictures of them," Zak said. "Quick."

Alex opened her phone and discreetly snapped a few shots. "Why am I doing this?" she asked through the side of her mouth.

"If you got the photos, get out of here."

Alex put down her phone and started the car.

"Turn right out of here," Zak said. "Don't go back right away."

"But we need wine," Alex said.

"We can't," Zak exclaimed. "Go. *Now*."

Hearing the anxiety in his voice, Alex pulled out of the parking lot. As she turned onto the main highway, Zak sat up.

"What's going on?" she asked as they headed out of town.

"What's your PIN?"

"9876. Why?"

Zak entered the numbers and looked at the photos she'd just taken. "Shit."

"What?" Alex asked. "What happened?"

Zak looked behind them, then at Alex. "Did any cars leave the parking lot?"

"No. I'm sure we're okay."

Zak pointed down the road to his left. "Make that left at the bottom of this hill."

Alex turned left off the highway and headed down Red Rock Loop Road.

"Just follow this road. It loops around back to the highway." Zak sat back. "We can make sure we're not being followed. And you might like the drive."

"Yeah, I know this road. I'd rather not be here."

Zak glanced behind them. "What's wrong with it?"

Alex kept her eyes forward. "I lived here with someone I was in love with." She sighed. "But like the story of my life, he wasn't in love with me."

"Oh, sorry. Where's he now?"

"That's the problem," Alex said, turning right and left around the curves. Each curve was like a stab of pain in her stomach. "I heard rumors he built a house back here. A huge monstrosity, so he could always look at Cathedral Rock."

"What's so important about Cathedral Rock?"

Alex pulled over as the major red rock vortex in Sedona came into view, its spires reaching to the heavens. Even though she didn't believe in the woo-woo energy stuff of Sedona, her chest always tightened when she got close to it.

"Skeater said it was his muse," Alex said. "And he wanted to be around it. He said it helped him produce number-one albums." She glanced at Zak. "But it always freaked me out."

"Why?"

"No idea," Alex replied. "Sometimes I'd feel this pressure in my chest or I'd get an urge to run away." She smiled briefly. "Like now." She put her hand to her heart. "I know it's silly, but I just don't like the thing." She glared at the vortex with disdain. "Still don't."

Alex pulled back onto the road. As they came around a bend, she gasped. "Damn. That has to be it."

Above them, built into the side and top of a red rock cliff, was an eyesore of a steel-and-glass mansion.

Alex stopped the car and looked up. "That abomination has to be Skeater's house. I heard he built it into the red rock, and it's ugly as shit."

They stared up at the mansion jutting out from the red stone.

"How does he get in there?" Alex mumbled.

"That red bit looks like an elevator," Zak said, leaning forward and pointing at part of the house. It rose from the rock like a fiery column. "Or up that cable?" He leaned back. "No one should be allowed to build like that."

"Yeah, well, that's Skeater. He created some number-one albums for a few top bands, made a ton of money, and turned into a complete asshole."

The knock on the window made Alex screech and jump in fright. She turned and saw the glass eyes of a well-worn ferret staring at her. "Fuck, no," fell out of her mouth. "It just keeps getting worse."

"What the...?" Zak started.

Alex lowered her window halfway. "Hi, Skeater."

An aging hippy of a man with an unshaven face, long gray-streaked hair, and aviator sunglasses peeked through the window. "Hey, Alex. I thought that was you. How you doing?"

She closed her eyes. "Never better. Busy running away from the bad guys."

Skeater laughed. "Yeah, yeah, you running away. Classic."

Alex glared out the window at him. "I wouldn't have left if I hadn't caught you fucking your intern. In *our bed*."

Skeater swayed from side to side. "Yeah, well, that was years ago. Youth. Stupidity. You know. All that." He shifted Skat to his other arm and leaned into the window again. "I'm clean now, you know. Doing the Steps and all that."

Alex kept her gaze straight ahead. "Good for you."

He shifted his stuffed pet to his other arm. "You here to see me?"

"No. Just driving through."

"Well, I Ninth Stepped you, but you never called back."

Anger boiled as Alex's hair turned black. She stared straight ahead. "You mean that voicemail where all you did was talk about yourself?"

"Yeah, man, the voicemail."

She felt Skeater's breath on her face as he leaned into the window. Every muscle in her body tensed until it hurt.

"I made amends," Skeater said. "You should be okay."

Alex squeezed her eyes shut. Through gritted teeth, she told him, "You never apologized for hurting me. You never said you were sorry for what you did to me. You never mentioned how you broke my heart." She opened her eyes and glared at him. "You talked about *you*. Like you always talked about you."

Skat's well-worn fur filled the window as the ferret bobbed back in front of her face. Skeater must have been hugging and petting his dead pet for decades.

"Yes, I did." He leaned back into the window. "I did the Steps. I'm good."

When he poked his head farther into the window, Alex pulled back and pressed herself into the seat.

"Oh, hey, man," Skeater said as he switched Skat to his other arm and thrust his hand toward Zak. "I'm Skeater."

Alex cursed herself for feeling the electricity as his arm grazed her shoulder. Something kicked her from inside her stomach. *No!* an internal voice screamed.

She pushed it down.

With a confused look, Zak shook Skeater's hand. "Zak."

Skeater pointed to Alex and Zak. "You two?"

"No," Zak said. "Just friends."

Alex saw the relief on Skeater's face. *Motherfucker.* She fumed at his inability to consider anyone else. He had screwed around on her, never cared about her or her feelings, and now stood there thinking he might have another chance. Alex would never let him back into her life.

Skeater pointed to his eyesore of a refuge. "Hey, wanna come up?"

Alex stared at him. "It's rather ugly, isn't it?"

"The house?" Skeater shifted his weight to the other side. "Yeah. I designed it while I was still doing drugs. Had no idea what I was thinking."

"Well, Tony Stark would love it," Zak said.

Skeater laughed. "Yeah, the Avengers and all that. I hear that a lot."

Zak chuckled politely.

Alex looked back and forth at the two men. Skeater had been her life for so many years. She'd hung off his every word and done everything he'd asked her to do. She would try to guess what he wanted and have it for him. But it was never enough. Why had she bent so far backward for him? Because she was in love. But was that love?

"Thanks, Skeater," Alex said. "But we can't come up. We're busy."

Skeater stepped back. She couldn't see his expression through his sunglasses, but Alex sensed his surprise. As she started to put up her window, she paused and glanced up at her first love. "I want to say it's nice to see you, Skeater, but you broke my heart. Like no one else ever has. Or ever will." She looked down the road then back toward him. "I hope you're happy."

Alex shut the window and put the car in drive. As she pulled away, she looked in the rearview mirror. Skeater stood in the middle of the road, shoulders drooping, a blanket of sadness covering him. His well-worn stuffed ferret was still tucked under his arm.

Alex was surprised she felt sorry for him. He looked so alone. Or perhaps she was being pulled into her past. She hated Skeater but was oddly drawn to him. *No!* she screamed silently to herself.

Alex and Zak pulled back onto the highway and headed toward the house.

"Do you want to...?" Zak started.

"No, I don't want to talk about it." She gripped the steering wheel and kept her eyes straight ahead, her hair a rainbow of confusion, frustration, and anger. "What I want is a drink."

Zak jumped at the ding. He pulled his phone from a side pocket of his cargo pants.

"You have a phone?" Alex asked. "Why didn't you just call for help when you were escaping?"

"Totally forgot I had it." Zak opened the cell. "And there wasn't any reception where we were, trust me." He looked at the text. "Wow. It's Max." He looked at Alex with surprise. "That's weird."

Alex shrugged. "Whatever. His ears were probably burning from everyone talking about him."

Zak read the message. "He says, *Need u. Know truth. On the run.*" He looked up. "We have to go back right away."

"But I need some booze," Alex said. "You have no idea."

Zak pointed down the highway. "Look ahead, a few lights down. It looks like a parking lot." He held up his phone. "This is beyond serious. *You* have no idea. Get us back now. I'll get you something later."

Grumbling, Alex turned at the light and headed back toward Boynton Canyon. Sedona wasn't a long-term option, nor was the band of misfits she'd found herself with.

When they reached the house, Zak rushed inside, a large bag of pastries, fruit, and coffee in each hand. Alex angrily followed.

He half threw the bags on the table. "You won't believe what happened."

Sharlene, Jackie, and Hank looked at him. He glanced around. "Where's Crystal?"

"Taking a shower," Sharlene said. "What's going on?"

"I don't want to wait for her," Zak said, then looked at Sharlene. "We saw Nate and Aaron, the guys who tried to kidnap me and Crystal."

"Where?" asked Jackie.

"At the bakery," Alex said, standing at the kitchen counter. "They were going inside after we'd gotten back to our car."

"They didn't—" Jackie started.

"No, they didn't see us." Alex pulled out her phone. "I took some photos of them, though." She unlocked her cell and dropped it on the table.

"Holy crap," Jackie said as she looked at the picture on Alex's screen.

"What?" everyone said in unison.

Just then, Crystal walked in, her hair wrapped in a bath towel. "What's going on?"

"Zak and Alex saw the people who kidnapped you," Sharlene said as Crystal approached the table.

"And that's Aaron Minor," Jackie exclaimed, holding the phone toward Crystal.

"Who?" Sharlene asked as Hank uttered a "holy shit."

"I didn't recognize him when we got Crystal," Hank said.

Alex sat up and leaned forward. "*The* Aaron Minor? I didn't notice with his baseball cap so low."

Jackie nodded. "*The* Aaron Minor. The tech guy who owns most of the world."

"No, that's Nate and Aaron," Crystal said as she looked at the images on Alex's cell.

Jackie held up her phone. On it was a media photo of Aaron. "This is the top tech person in the world. He's worth billions and billions."

Crystal toweled off her wet hair and stepped back. She shook her mane and styled it into place with her fingers. "Why would one of the richest people in the world kidnap me?"

"Probably the same reason JT's trying to get you," Jackie offered.

"But why would someone like him personally kidnap me? Wouldn't he have someone else do it?" Crystal asked.

"This is totally him," Jackie said. "He's eccentric. He'll work customer service phones at one of his companies or show up in a restaurant bussing tables. In interviews, he's said he wants to stay connected to reality, so he often does things himself. I'm not surprised he showed up in person."

"But he could get arrested for kidnapping," Crystal said.

Sharlene smiled her grandmotherly smile. "Sweetie, people like him are never held responsible for what they do."

"You're right," said Jackie. "He says he enjoys being with 'the people,' but he still wants all the privileges of the elite."

Alex smiled to herself; there was nothing wrong with that.

"More important," Sharlene said, "how did Aaron Minor know Crystal was in Sedona?"

"Shit," Hank said. "They bugged you." He jumped up and rushed toward Crystal. "Where are your clothes? Everything you had on."

"Um, upstairs on the bathroom floor." Crystal looked down at herself. "These are spare clothes from here." She pointed to her feet. "Oh, except my Converse. I wore them."

Hank started for the stairs but stopped. He turned back. "Your shoes. They'd put a tracking device in there in case you escaped. You'd take your shoes with you." He walked over to Crystal. "Take them off." He turned to Zak. "Your shoes too."

Crystal kicked off her shoes. "Please don't ruin them."

Hank grabbed her sneakers and Zak's hiking boots and rushed to the living area. "I should have known," he said as he felt the canvas. "Minor must have bugged you in the van." He inspected the bottom rubber, then searched the inside footbed. Hank dropped the left sneaker and inspected the right one. As he pushed on the interior cushioning, he stopped. He gently lifted the insole and scratched at the footbed.

"Yes," he said, pulling out a tiny microchip. He dropped the shoe and grabbed Zak's boots, thoroughly searching them. He pulled out a chip from the inside footbed on the right shoe.

Hank ran out the front door.

The sound of pounding floated into the room, along with Hank's angry grunts. He reappeared and put the smashed electronics on the table.

"Sorry, Sharlene," Hank said, grabbing Crystal and Zak's shoes and returning them. "I should have known."

"Now, now," Sharlene replied. "It's no one's fault. You took care of it."

"Should we move?" Jackie asked.

Sharlene sighed. "I don't want to, but we'll probably need to. At least the safeguards here at the house protect us from being discovered." She looked at their one-man security force. "Can you monitor things carefully, Hank?"

With a nod, Hank pulled out his phone.

"I'll get a place lined up," Jackie said as she stood. "Just in case."

"Sorry, everyone," Zak said. "Not trying to interrupt, but something else happened." He took out his phone. "Max texted."

A collective gasp filled the room.

"Wait," Crystal said. "You have a phone?"

"No reception in the desert," Alex said disdainfully, still angry she couldn't get a drink. "Oh, and he forgot he had it." She leaned against the kitchen counter, arms crossed.

"I did forget," Zak replied. "You know, not everyone's addicted to their phone." He shook his head. "Doesn't matter." He opened the message. "Max said, *Need u. Know truth. On the run.*"

Sharlene patted the table and sat back. "Finally. Some good news." She looked at the others. "What should we do?"

Hank pulled a croissant from a bag. "Let's lure him to a truck stop somewhere and bring him in." He bit into the buttery pastry.

Zak turned to him. "I know you're a military guy and all, but how about we meet him somewhere and invite him back here?"

Hank shook his head. "I think the bump on your head is worse than we thought."

Zak glanced around the table. "I know Max. He's a good guy. He'd probably faint at the sight of a gun pointed at him."

"And he might work with the people going after Crystal." Hank shoved the last of the pastry into his mouth and licked his fingers.

Zak shook his head. "If he's on the run, he's not working with them. He's running away from them."

"How about this?" Sharlene said. "Text him back, Zak. Tell him we'll contact him again in a few minutes from another number."

Zak nodded and replied to Dr. Max.

Sharlene slid her chair back and opened a drawer by the fridge. She pulled out their burner. "Hank, let's figure out a truck stop to meet him at. You, Jackie, and Zak go get him." She powered up the phone and gave Hank a serious look. "And you'll be nice to him."

Jackie leaned back. "And if he seems like a hostile, you can shoot his kneecaps and kidnap him." She smiled as Hank let out a grunt.

Alex slipped quietly from the room.

Chapter Eight

A week after Crystal disappeared, an anal explosion of epic proportions bubbled and gurgled in JT's gut. The pressure quickly mounted to eruptive levels.

"Wait!" he screamed into his cell phone. He muted the line and dashed into his executive washroom. He squeezed his cheeks as tightly as he could and lunged for the heated, gold-plated seat. As his rear made contact, an explosive force of maximum magnitude erupted out his ass, shooting him three feet in the air. JT's insides filled the bowl and spilled over the sides. The automatic flush and bidet spray couldn't keep up with the quantity of excrement being released from his intestines.

He groaned and gagged while gingerly stepping away from the bowl. When his erect penis released its contents into his mess, he sighed with relief and release.

JT raced into his executive shower and cleaned himself off. Minutes later he was back at his desk, private cell phone in hand and ass warm, dry, and clean.

He punched his intercom. "Get Five in here. Venting incident in the washroom, level ten." He paused. "Or twelve." He unmuted his private cell phone. "What the hell did you say?"

"I thought you died," came out in a long Texan drawl.

"So did I," JT mumbled. He glanced up briefly as a hazmat suit with full breathing apparatus snuck by him. JT spun around in his chair and looked out his window. He reminded himself that if he didn't see it, it didn't exist.

"McMahon," JT barked. "What the hell did you say?"

"Well," McMahon drawled, "I've got The Society's not-so-legal satellites and top tech folk on the case."

There was a pause as JT heard the sounds of cigar sucking. McMahon continued. "Aaron Minor tried to kidnap your asset. He was trying to steal your technology."

The lightsaber fight of all time would begin shortly. It might be a store-bought sword for the moment, but JT needed to slay the demons that haunted him. Fortunately, he had nothing left in his stomach to expel. He popped some stormtrooper tabs to be sure and washed them down with his ever-present processed protein shake.

"That little shit," he said, then took another sip.

"Agree," McMahon replied. "Little pimply-faced prick. Want my men to deal with him?"

"Oh, no," JT responded. "I'll take care of him myself."

The sucking sounds paused. "And I still get access to the technology for helping you?"

JT clenched his fists as he kept his voice calm. "Yes, Sam. I'll hold up my end of the deal. After I can control the energy."

He made a mental note to never learn how his invention worked.

McMahon grunted with greedy satisfaction. "We could fuck The Society and do our own thing. Keep future Minors from getting near us."

"I'll think about it. Where's the tech asshole now?"

"Sedona. Where hippies go to die." McMahon let out a deep, throaty, congested laugh.

JT grunted and clicked off his cell, then pressed his intercom button. "One, get my jet ready. The Gulfstream. We're going to Arizona. And I hope you have all the intel on that missing test subject. You're coming with me."

JT sat back. They'd confirmed it. McMahon and The Society's super-elite security force had gathered proof that the pasty little dweeb Minor was trying to steal JT's work. Or sabotage him. Or both.

He grasped his lightsaber and cut through the air, fighting the evil that had haunted him since birth. When he was sufficiently exhausted, he hit his intercom again. "Get me to the airport now. We're going to Sedona." He took a long swig of his processed protein drink as One of Five appeared in his office and grabbed his briefcase shoulder bag.

Super wealth had many advantages, one of them being ease of travel. No checkpoints, no lines, no public to get messy with. And with billionaire wealth, JT could get to the super-secret private airport just outside New York City in fifteen minutes. His private helicopter, parked on the roof of his building, made sure of that.

Within an hour, JT and One of Five were taking off in his Gulfstream. Once they were airborne, JT called back to his top assistant. One of Five raced to the commercial economy plane seat across from the leather sofa where JT was lounging.

"Yes, sir."

"Give me the report."

"Do you want everything or...?"

JT glared. "How stupid are you?" He sipped his gin and tonic. One of Five hadn't been offered anything to drink, even water, because working for JT was a privilege, not a party.

One fumbled through his bag.

"That thing that's gone missing."

"Oh." One pulled out his iPad and summarized the report. "Her name is Crystal. She was with another woman. The vehicle was registered to a Finn Klein of Klein Design Strategies. It's a marketing company your company Wilson Industries owns."

"You don't say," JT said. "What else?"

One scrolled to the next section. "The woman in the car was Alexandra Scott, or Alex, as everyone calls her. She worked at Klein Strategies, but Klein fired her not too long ago." One continued to skim the report. "Seems Ms. Scott had both worked for and been engaged to Klein, but he broke off the engagement and fired her."

"Now that's interesting."

The assistant continued to share the report with JT, who was half listening.

JT looked up from his solitaire game. "Wait, what did you just say?"

One of Five looked up from his screen. "Just now?"

"Back a bit. The part you just started reading."

The assistant scrolled back, "Um, the worldwide network part?"

JT nodded.

"Over the past couple of years, a worldwide network has formed to help the spirits. It's called the Spiritual Enterprise Network, headed by Sharlene Montgomery."

The billionaire leaned back and sipped his drink. "That's even more interesting. Show me her photo."

One turned his device. A smiling Sharlene looked back at him, her brightly colored muumuu flowing about her as she walked on a beach.

"Why didn't anyone tell me about this?"

"They've been under surveillance, but your team didn't need to involve you. Nothing's happened yet."

"Unacceptable. Have the security team send me weekly reports about all threats to my operations. *All* of them."

One looked down. "Will do."

"What's this group doing?"

Slowly, JT's assistant scrolled through the report. He summarized, "It's a worldwide group that's trying to get the spirits back to their dimension." He scrolled further. "And it seems they're attempting to discover how to stop your energy extractions from happening, but they haven't tried anything yet."

"And that's not important enough to tell me?"

One looked blankly at his boss.

JT's eyes narrowed. "Fire whoever didn't tell me this sooner. This is a disgrace." He put down his drink. "My staff should know what I need before I do."

"Yes, sir."

JT picked up his cocktail and sat back as he considered his options. His original plan was to take the spirit to the lab, but waiting might be better. Perhaps the Network had technology he could profit from, or maybe their research would help solve his extraction problems. Spying on them first could end up being extremely profitable. He could kidnap the spirit any time.

"Show me that woman from the company I own." Because his employees were so incompetent, JT would do this himself.

One of Five held his iPad in front of JT.

Yes, JT thought as he looked at a recent Facebook photo of Alex and her wildly improbable hair. He studied the picture. She was smiling, but when he looked into her emerald green eyes, he saw the sadness and sensed her stress. Being fired by her ex-fiancé had definitely left scars.

This was his mark. It was much easier to control someone when they were knocked down, and JT was confident he could manipulate her to get anything he wanted.

Within several hours, JT was on the ground in Arizona. Three private contractors on loan from The Society for Advanced Economics met him at his plane. They had a military-style haircut, but they could have blended in anywhere and been mistaken for anyone. They were of average height, build, hair color, and even demeanor. They themselves were camouflage.

The lead mercenary snapped to attention. "Shooter, sir," he said as JT stepped off the plane. He turned to his team. "This is Pop, and that's Trigger."

The other two straightened and gave slight nods. JT walked by and ignored them as One of Five gave a short wave and a quiet hello. As they all drove down the mesa where the small private airport was located, Shooter turned to JT. "Sir, we've located Minor and the target."

JT looked up from his phone as he and One sat in the third row of the vehicle. "Good. What's next?"

"Minor's being lured to a private spot. He thinks he's meeting the asset. You can speak with him there." The private contractor started to turn away but stopped and glanced back. "We can eliminate any threat, sir. Just give the word."

"Good." JT nodded. "Also, change in plans."

"Yes, sir."

Shooter and Trigger turned toward him as Pop glanced in the rearview mirror.

The global kingpin put down his phone. "Minor's a priority, but we're going to wait before doing anything with the subject. I need more information on the group. And I might lure someone from the Network instead of kidnapping the asset."

"Yes, sir," barked all three ex-military guards.

"If my way doesn't work, we can bring her in."

"Yes, sir," rang through the car.

JT turned to One. "Why don't you talk to me like that?"

One looked up from his phone. "Uh, sorry, sir?"

"From now on, you 'yes, sir' me like those men just did."

"Okay."

JT glared at One.

"Yes, sir," exploded from One's mouth.

"Tell the others," JT said, a satisfied tingle tickling his loins.

The SUV drove into the far reaches of the red rocks, past Boynton Canyon and back toward several Native American heritage sites. The pavement disappeared, and the car bounced over a rutted road. They pulled into a red dirt trailhead parking area that was empty except for one other vehicle.

They parked away from the Jeep. JT laughed at Minor's stupidity. Only one bodyguard sat next to the tech giant.

Aaron Minor leapt out of the car, his arms doing their Gumby dance. Joy covered his face. His bodyguard, Nate, followed closely behind.

JT stepped out of the blacked-out SUV and watched with glee as Minor's childish grin quickly disappeared. The three mercenaries in all black followed JT. They trained their guns on Minor and his bodyguard. One of Five got out last, carrying a duffel bag.

The tech genius squeaked as JT stretched to his full five-foot-five height.

The global kingpin glared at his fellow Society member. "Aaron Minor, funny seeing you here."

Minor's eyes darted back and forth as his hands swayed in the air.

JT laughed his practiced evil laugh. "There's nowhere to go, Minor. My men can trample you in a second." He waved an arm toward the tech genius. "And put your damn hands down. This isn't a holdup. You need to get that problem fixed."

Aaron Minor put his arms down and shifted nervously from side to side. "Do we need all this security?" he asked, his air dancer routine underway as his uncontrollable arms flapped toward JT's guards. "We're just having a chat, aren't we?"

JT walked toward him and stopped an arm's length away. "No, we're not just having a chat." He looked at One and snapped his fingers. His assistant unzipped the bag as he walked to JT's side.

Minor started hopping in place, annoying JT even more.

"You tried to kidnap my property. And you're trying to steal my technology." JT took a step closer, so he was in the tech guru's face. "What do you say to that?"

Minor made a nervous sound—part chuckle, part moan. "What are you talking about? I'm here buying a place."

JT pulled a gun-looking device from One's open bag. Although this wasn't the exact extractor that had brought Crystal to earth, it was the first working prototype built at a smaller scale. The glitches his product designers had found had been fixed in future models. He waved it toward Minor's nose. "Is this what you're looking for?"

The tech genius's eyes widened as he stared at the device. "I told you, I'm here house hunting."

"My ass. You're trying to steal my property."

Minor shook his head, his light-brown baby curls swinging back and forth. His nondescript eyes greedily stared at the device. "No, no, no."

JT examined the extractor, turning it back and forth in his hand. "Yeah, it's gorgeous, isn't it? I call it the Cosmic Cannon. Junior." He looked at the tech giant. "The real one is at one of my secret labs." He lowered the device to his side. "Tell me why you want it."

Minor's eyes were fixated on the device. "I don't know what you're talking about."

JT's muscles tightened as gas collected in his bowels. "Don't fucking lie to me. I've told McMahon what you're doing. The Society could kill you for breaking the agreement."

Minor visibly shook. Tears filled his eyes. "I just… I…" His voice tapered off as he looked at JT. His arms and legs restarted their nervous air dancer routine. "You know I love technology. I'm fascinated by it. I just wanted to see how it works. That's all."

JT snorted. "Well, you're never going to. And I'm reporting you to the others at The Society. You've no right stealing my things."

Aaron Minor lunged for JT's gun. He grabbed JT's arm and tried to wrestle the device away. JT yanked back hard. They struggled.

The Cosmic Cannon discharged before any of the bodyguards could intervene. JT might or might not have forgotten he'd set the gun to kill. And he would never remember if he'd locked it after he'd played with it last.

The tech giant froze and fell to the ground with a thud. His limbs went stiff and were finally subdued.

"Whoops," JT said a little too gleefully. He looked at his weapon then at Aaron's frozen body.

As Nate reached for his gun, all three of JT's security team stepped forward, their revolvers still drawn and now pointed at Nate's head.

"I wouldn't if I were you," JT said, walking over to Minor's body. He kicked the stiff corpse.

Nate growled but remained silent.

JT looked at his team. "Let's get out of here."

The billionaire, One of Five, and the private contractors rushed back to the SUV. Shooter kept his gun trained on Nate. As they pulled away, JT watched Nate drag Minor to the Jeep. The last he saw of the tech genius was his frozen body being unceremoniously thrown into the backseat of the open-air car. His rigid legs stuck awkwardly out the back of the vehicle, like a discarded mannequin.

JT's team would clean up any potential police mess—though no one would ever prove the global kingpin was responsible for Minor's demise; his lawyers would make sure of that.

As JT got into his car, he finally understood his true power. He decided who lived and who died. The billionaire smiled his first truly satiated smile in years. He *would* rule them all.

***

Alex closed the door to her room and crumpled on the bed. The others could figure out how to find Zak's friend; she wasn't interested in any of it. Running into Skeater had brought back too many painful memories.

She stared at the ceiling, wondering what she'd done to deserve the pain that constantly rained down on her. As a child and teen, Alex believed someone or something was punishing her for her sins from a past life. She believed she'd done something so terrible and been such an evil person that even a Higher Power couldn't forgive her.

As the years went by and her hope for a successful and happy life slowly faded with each disappointment and heartbreak, Alex decided that there was no Higher Power. Skeater, Finn, her childhood, and currently being homeless with strange people who were chasing supposed celestial beings: the common denominator in her life experiences was her, so she must be the problem.

Alex didn't need any other force or entity to make her feel worthless and irredeemable. She could do that to herself.

She put her hand over her eyes, trying not to cry the angry tears fighting to get out. They didn't deserve her. None of them. And she couldn't forgive any of them. Not her parents for never being there, not the kids at school who'd bullied her for years, not the men in her life who'd abused her on so many levels. Alex fell into a fitful, angry sleep.

A few hours later, she opened her eyes and stretched. She had nothing to do except stare at the wall. And blame herself.

"What I need," Alex muttered as she propped herself up on her elbow, "is a drink." She swung her feet over the side of the bed and sighed.

The knock at her door pissed her off. Why couldn't they give her space? "Leave me alone," she said.

The door cracked open. "It's me," said Sharlene. "The others are getting the scientist, and I wanted to make sure you're okay. Can I come in?"

"I'm not in the mood," Alex replied.

Sharlene opened the door and slipped inside.

"I'm *really* not in the mood," Alex repeated, her hair streaking an even darker black.

Gingerly, Sharlene sat on the side of the bed next to her. "Do you want to talk, sweetie?"

Alex glared at her. "What don't you understand about me not wanting to talk?" She jerked away as the older woman reached out to touch her. "Geezus, leave me alone."

Sharlene lowered her hand. "Alex. Something's obviously bothering you. Why don't you talk about it? You'll feel better."

Alex stood up. "I don't want to talk. Or want your help." She started for the door but stopped and looked at Sharlene. "I don't want to be here." She turned her back to the network head. "And maybe I don't fucking care."

She stormed from the room, her hair a rainbow of anger black, stress magenta, and dark green disgust. She raced down the stairs and grabbed the car keys. If Alex didn't find a drink in the next five minutes, she'd lose her mind.

She jumped into the spare car and sped out of Boynton Canyon. She slowed as she neared the main highway. A huge sigh of relief escaped her mouth.

Alex turned left onto 89A and inched her way to uptown Sedona, where most of the shops and tourists were. And bars. But with the increasing popularity of the town year-round, the two-lane highway was more often like a stalled Los Angeles freeway at rush hour than a quiet desert oasis.

When her hair turned nearly all black, she knew she couldn't wait. Alex veered to the right and pulled into the parking lot of the first restaurant she saw.

"Oh, fuck no!" she screamed as she nearly pulled into Chocola Tree, the town's organic raw vegan, macrobiotic height-of-woo-woo spot. She jerked back onto the highway, ignoring the cars that honked at her.

When she saw a steakhouse sign, she pulled in. "I'll eat raw cow before I have any more cardboard," she said as she got out and slammed the door. There was only so much homemade vegan granola a person could stomach.

After finding a booth, she ordered two double Jack Daniels and opened the menu. When the drinks arrived, she downed the first one in a gulp and sighed. As the liquid settled into her bloodstream, her muscles relaxed. In less than a minute, she felt the temporary peace of the first drink.

Alex picked up the second glass and looked at the amber liquid. She sighed. Nothing was better than the first drink or two. Every cell in her body would relax and her troubles would disappear. She vowed to control herself.

She pulled out her personal phone and noticed she'd left it turned on. Alex took a large swallow from the second glass and opened the menu. She realized she wasn't in the mood for steak—she'd have less room to drink.

Salad and French fries, she thought. Balance the good and the bad. She realized she was fooling herself. Fries were good enough. And onion rings.

Alex ordered a beer to go along with her whiskey. She hadn't had a drink in quite a while, so she knew she needed to slow down. And beer wasn't really alcohol.

She sat back and relaxed, then looked around at the ample-waisted tourists and sun-weathered locals having dinner. She finished her second Jack.

She busied herself looking at her phone. She couldn't let the tourists, who were completely oblivious to her, think she was a loser. Because she believed she was.

The sound of a glass clunking onto her table startled her. She looked up, expecting to see the server.

Alex's mouth fell open in shock.

"Hi, Alex." JT pushed her beer toward her.

"You're JT," she stuttered.

JT laughed. "Yes, yes, I am." He sat across from her in the booth, then grabbed the stormtrooper PEZ dispenser from his pocket and knocked back a few candies.

"Mind if I join you," he stated, rather than asked, as he crunched loudly. He grabbed the menu the hostess had left behind and opened it. A moment later, JT snapped his fingers to get the server's attention.

Alex was shocked that Jackson Thomas Wilson, one of the world's richest men, knew her name and was sitting across from her.

JT put in his order and tossed a couple more goodies from his stormtrooper dispenser into his mouth. As he crunched, he said, "So you know me."

Alex nodded.

"Well, I've had my eye on you for a while," he said.

She had trouble keeping her mouth closed. "You don't know me. And how did you find me?"

JT laughed with arrogant entitlement. "I'm the phone company you use."

"But you have no idea who I am."

JT sipped the vodka that appeared in front of him, grimacing slightly. The restaurant obviously didn't serve the top-shelf booze he was used to.

"I know all my employees," he said.

"You've got the wrong person. I'm not your employee." Alex took a long swig of beer. Already fuzzy headed, she focused on staying present. "I'm nobody."

JT sat back, his stubby fingers drumming the table. He flinched and stopped. He rubbed his hands together and sniffed his fingers, nearly gagging from the smell. "Lovely dive bar you found."

Alex looked at him with growing contempt. "Don't be an ass."

JT tilted his head and laughed loudly. He lowered his gaze, his black eyes boring holes into Alex. The combination of a smile and dead eyes meant danger. Finn and her father had taught her that. She backed down.

"Lovely way to greet someone," JT said.

Alex took another large swallow of beer. "You've got the wrong person."

He put down his vodka. "How's Finn?"

Alex's mouth fell open again.

"He and that young little thing had the baby, I hear. Premature. But a healthy baby boy. They were so happy when you left without a fuss."

A knife stabbed Alex in the stomach. "That asshole fired me. What was I supposed to do?" She grabbed her beer and took another long drink, nearly emptying the glass.

JT snapped at the server and pointed to Alex's pint and whiskey glasses. With money comes power and often misguided, entitled rudeness. The server would put up with JT's arrogant abuse in order to keep her job.

"I own Finn's company."

Alex flinched. "What?"

JT sat back with a smug look. "I own a lot of things. Klein Design Strategies was bought a year ago by a subsidiary of JTW Corporate called Wilson Industries."

"But you're ShopMe."

JT laughed. "I'm so much more than one company. I started with ShopMe, but I now own dozens of businesses. And they all fall under the JTW Corporate umbrella. Like Wilson Industries, which now owns Klein Strategies."

Alex shook her head. "I don't understand."

JT leaned forward and flashed a quick, spine-chilling smile. "Well, let's put it this way. I own your ex-fiancé and ex-boss, Finn."

Alex reeled. Finn had never told her. But of course he wouldn't. He probably pocketed millions from the sale. And had hidden it from her. The knife dug in deeper.

"That's why I'm here." JT sat back against the red vinyl booth and looked around. "What in the world are you doing in the middle of nowhere?"

"I ask myself that question every hour," Alex mumbled. She nodded her thanks as the server placed another round of drinks on the table. Alex stared at the full glass of beer and double whiskey, past caring and over her tipping point. She'd stop drinking tomorrow.

She finished the last swallow of her first beer and pushed the pint glass aside. Her tongue loosened as her thoughts became slippery.

She sipped her second pint and put it down. "You still haven't told me why you're here."

She looked at JT. His cold eyes stared deep into her. She shuddered. He covered his angry malevolence with a plastic smile.

JT sipped his vodka and smacked his lips. "I've been looking for you."

Alex let out a snort-laugh. "Whatever you say." She held her beer toward JT. "Here's to liars and assholes." She took a gulp and put down her glass.

JT's eyes hungrily roamed Alex's body. An electric shock ran through her as she shivered with a combination of titillation and disgust. *No, no, no!* she screamed to herself as a wet warmth pulsated between her legs.

JT looked at her, his expression blank. Alex couldn't read him. He looked like he was having a private debate with himself.

Food appeared before them. A huge piece of sirloin for JT. Fries and onion rings for Alex. She poured ketchup on her fries and mustard next to her rings.

JT snapped his fingers. A tall, thin, nervous-looking young man sprang from behind a wooden beam, a leather bag slung across his shoulder.

He jumped to JT's side and handed him a tumbler with a straw sticking out. JT sipped the drink as the stranger quickly cut the tycoon's steak into bite-size pieces. He disappeared as quickly as he had come.

"Who…?" Alex started.

"My assistant. Nobody."

JT took a bite of the red, juicy animal muscle. "Not bad for a dump like this."

Alex shook her head but stayed quiet. He was probably baiting her. Men like him always had to win.

She took another gulp of beer. "Again, what are you doing here?"

JT held up a hunk of meat on his fork and twirled it back and forth. "I'm here to offer you a job, Alex."

Alex nearly spat out her fries. She coughed and sipped more beer. "You what?"

JT stuffed the hunk of meat into his mouth. While chewing, he said, "I'm here to offer you a job." Bits of steak bounced up and down in his mouth as he spoke. "Finn had no right to fire the best employee he had. The best employee *I* had. I need people like you."

Alex's jaw dropped; nothing would come out.

JT leaned forward, his smarmy eyes on fire. "Let's fuck Finn."

Alex couldn't close her mouth.

He stabbed another hunk of meat and chewed noisily. Cow juices dripped down his chin. His assistant appeared and quickly wiped JT's mouth, then vanished behind the beam with the soiled napkin.

"I want you to work at my new casino JW in Las Vegas."

Alex could barely form a "What?"

"I want you to head up and run the experiential marketing division. Events, parties, campaigns—that sort of thing—to promote the casino."

Alex couldn't believe her ears. This was the job she'd always wanted. "Seriously?"

JT nodded. "You'll get two fifty a year, plus expenses and bonus."

Alex shook her head. She was hearing things. "Excuse me?"

JT spoke slowly, enunciating each word. "Two hundred and fifty thousand dollars a year in salary, plus expenses and an annual bonus." He stabbed another piece of meat. "And a signing bonus." He looked at her and smiled. "Obviously."

Alex kicked herself under the table to make sure she was awake. This was her dream come true, and it would piss the fuck out of Finn. And she could get out of Sedona.

JT put his elbows on the table and clasped his hands, his eyes glued to her breasts. "Well?"

Alex felt hints of sadistic evil seeping from his pores, and a little voice in her gut screamed, *No*. But it was so much money. And it would kill Finn. She shifted in her seat as throbbing waves of greed spread from her inner thighs to her chest.

She could also get away from Skeater. This explained the hell she'd gone through over the past several months—and her life.

JT pushed aside his plate and popped a few more tabs from the dispenser. "I have to know now, Alex. And you have to come with me. There's still a lot of work to be done before the casino officially opens."

Alex knocked back her whiskey and gagged her internal voice. This opportunity would never come again. She nodded. "I'll take it."

"Let's celebrate."

JT didn't even snap this time. He yelled across the restaurant and had two double whiskeys brought over.

Once the drinks were on the table, he waved his hand. His assistant jumped back to his side. He opened his shoulder bag, pulled out a stack of papers, and placed them in front of Alex. Sticky notes peeked out from various pages.

The assistant handed Alex a pen. As she took it from him, she saw the fear in his eyes. They darted right, left, right, left, like he was saying, "No," trying to warn her.

Alex ignored him. She'd never get this chance again, and she wouldn't blow things this time.

JT pointed to the contract. "Sign where all the Post-its are." He handed her a whiskey. "And let's toast your new job."

Alex took the Jack Daniels and picked up the pen.

"Drink up." JT saluted her with his glass and sipped the vodka he still had. Smacking his lips, he motioned for her to drink.

Alex knew better. She heard the voice in her gut. She shouldn't sign anything half drunk.

JT kept motioning for her to drink.

Alex looked him in the eye and thought, *Fuck it*. She knocked back the glass and pulled the papers in front of her, then paused.

JT slid the second glass of whiskey to her side of the table. "Now, Alex. There's so much work to do."

"I should read this, though." She looked down and found the words swimming on the page.

JT pointed to the Jack he'd just put in front of her. "Drink," he commanded.

Alex looked at the glass, then at the global kingpin.

He reached over and slid it closer to her. "I said drink."

Alex stared at him, her hair streaking anger black. She picked up the glass and downed it.

JT grabbed her wrist and squeezed hard. "No one in the history of business has ever read an employment contract. They're all the same."

Alex shivered with delight and disgust. She screamed inside for her body to stop.

JT slid his hand down and roughly pinched the soft skin on her inner arm. "Sign it."

She gasped and looked at her arm in bewilderment. Her body vibrated with desire.

Alex looked up and saw a satisfied smirk on JT's face. Her growing lust disgusted her.

"And you'll get a hundred thousand as a signing bonus."

Alex's mouth fell open. "Excuse me?"

He nodded. "One hundred thousand dollars in your bank account as soon as you sign." He sat back. "I already have your account info in the system, so the money's yours the second you sign."

"You have my bank account information?"

JT smiled. "I know everything about you. All your personal info is already in my system."

Alex felt an ominous cloud of caution hang over her. She looked at the papers. She'd have money again, and she wouldn't have to spend another day with Sharlene and her group of misfits. And maybe she would fuck JT. So what? This would definitely drive Finn crazy. She leaned over and signed all the pages.

When the last signature was in place, the assistant appeared at the table.

"One, this is Alex. She'll be working in Vegas."

One of Five nodded and reached down for the papers. Alex noticed him staring at her, his eyeballs still darting right, left, right, left.

She looked away and grabbed the fresh glass of whiskey that had mysteriously appeared in front of her. She breathed deeply as the room began to tilt.

One put the papers back in his bag and disappeared behind the beam.

"Congratulations, Alex. You're now one of us."

A wave of fear flashed across her, mixed with the leftover sting of desire from JT's pinch. She downed the alcohol in two gulps.

"Oh, hell no," shot across the restaurant. Alex turned to see Sharlene storming across the space, her orange muumuu flapping about her. "She is *not* yours."

Whiskey backwashed into Alex's mouth. She swallowed it quickly before it sprayed across the table. It seemed the sweet grandmother of goodness had a temper.

JT turned to Sharlene and laughed. "You must be Sharlene, the great wonder of Sedona and caretaker to my new friend here, Alex." He looked her up and down. "My researchers had you pegged." He leaned toward her and stage-whispered. "Your muumuu gave you away."

Alex looked from JT to Sharlene, her mind a mixture of whiskey and beer. The room spun.

JT grabbed his briefcase and stood. "Alex, it's time to go."

"Alex," Sharlene said softly. "What have you done?"

Alex looked at Sharlene's sensible, orthopedic-looking sandals, unable to find words. "I had to," she muttered to the floor.

JT put his sweaty hand around her wrist and pulled her up from the table. "Come with me."

Sharlene grabbed Alex's other arm. "Alex, don't go. Please. Don't go."

The alcohol hit Alex full force when she stood. "I couldn't say no," she slurred, head still down. "And I can't stay here. Skeater. Finn." She looked in Sharlene's direction as she swayed back and forth. "And you all."

JT laughed. "She's mine, Miss Sharlene. Already signed the contract."

Sharlene let go of Alex's arm. Alex saw the shock on her face.

"Alex, you'll regret this."

Alex shakily stepped backward and slurred, "Can't regret it any more than the past forty-five years of my life."

Roughly, JT tugged on her arm and squeezed until it hurt. He pulled her toward the door. Alex stumbled forward, nearly losing her balance.

"Be happy, Sharlene," Alex slurred, turning back and waving at her. "I'm rich." She tripped and caught herself. "And I'll finally be happy."

Sharlene stood still, slowly shaking her head.

Chapter Nine

Hank pulled up to headquarters in a Prius, a passenger and two excited dogs in the seat next to him. Jackie and Zak followed in the Range Rover. They all walked into the house.

Sharlene moved away from the window and met them in the hall. "Oh, thank goodness," she said. She smiled warmly as she saw the additions to their group.

Hank handed the two squirming, long-haired chihuahuas to her. "Take these, please."

Sharlene's face lit up. "Well, who are these two cuties?" she asked as she took the two dogs and held them close. They both reached up to lick her cheeks.

"Fred and George," the stranger replied as he nervously shifted from foot to foot, his mushroom cloud hair swaying back and forth.

"This is Dr. Max from the lab," Zak said. "He's here to help."

Sharlene nodded and walked with the dogs into the kitchen. The rest followed. "We'll get you two adorable pups some water, won't we?" she said as she put them down and rummaged for some bowls. They stayed at her feet, their tails doing a happy dance.

"Where's Crystal?" Jackie asked.

Sharlene pointed to the other side of the room. "She's not well, so she's lying down."

"Is it getting worse?"

Sharlene nodded. "She's phasing in and out almost all the time and often disappears completely for a second or two."

Dr. Max put his hand to his forehead. "I'm so sorry. I had no idea."

"It's fine," Zak said. "Have a seat. You didn't know, did you?"

Dr. Max took a seat at the table. "But I should have."

Sharlene brought over a tray of glasses and a pitcher of iced tea as everyone sat. She then joined the group.

"Can you fill me in on what's happening?" Sharlene asked as she poured iced tea and passed around her vegan oatmeal cookies.

"I learned the truth about the experiments right before I texted Zak," Dr. Max said. "And it's not to cure amnesia like I was told." He glanced around the table. "I really believed the subjects had amnesia."

He picked up Fred and put him in his lap. "Some of my staff tried to tell me," he continued. "Even Zak. But I didn't believe anyone until a couple of days ago. I pulled all the research together, and it wasn't what I was told." He gave his dog a quick scratch behind the ears. "I was so blinded by my work."

Jackie nodded. "Well, you're helping us now. Crystal needs to get back where she belongs. She's getting worse. We're afraid she'll disappear completely soon."

"That makes sense," Dr. Max said. "It's like a battery being drained. She doesn't have much juice left."

"It just dawned on me," Sharlene said. "Crystal ran out of gum, and I couldn't get her any yet. She started getting worse than usual after that." She looked at Dr. Max. "Could the gum help her somehow?"

The scientist shook his head slowly. "I'm not sure. The sugar or the titanium dioxide or some other chemical might increase her quantum energy." He added, "I'm not an expert, but if it helps her, keep giving it to her. It could be why she hasn't phased out completely. She's lasted longer than the other subjects who came through." He lowered his head. "I was told they were moved in the middle of the night, not that they were fading from existence." Dr. Max shifted in his chair. "Also, it seems the way these spirits come to earth is affecting the space-time continuum. And not in a good way."

Sharlene's eyes widened. "Our scientists have been afraid of that."

Jackie looked from Sharlene to Dr. Max. "What do you mean?"

"If what I uncovered in the lab files is true," the scientist said, "it's bad. A researcher came in for a couple months and wouldn't tell us why she was there. But I was able to break into her files a couple days ago. She reported that the process that makes the spirits fall to earth and disappear is creating mini black holes that are folding in on themselves. Eventually, they could create a massive one that could destroy the planet and possibly the universe."

Sharlene put her hand over her heart. "Our team thought something more serious was happening, but none of them considered this." She looked around the table, her hands shaking. "I can't believe it. This isn't just about Crystal, even though we want her safe. This is about the destruction of our space-time continuum and everything in it."

Hank looked around the table. "Isn't that a bit much?"

Dr. Max shook his head. "You don't mess with quantum fields and inter-dimensionality. No one fully understands them. This is very serious." He shifted in his seat. "And I might have worse news. And it's even more grim."

"What could be worse than that?" asked Sharlene.

"The researcher had a hypothesis." Dr. Max put Fred down. "She was concerned spirits weren't the only thing disappearing. She believed the humans they were connected to would eventually die because of the disconnection."

A collective gasp sounded throughout the room.

"Holy shit," fell out of Jackie's mouth.

"'Grim' is definitely an understatement," Sharlene said.

Dr. Max gently tapped on the table. "I know. Let's hope it's only a theory."

"Has anyone started looking into it?" Hank asked.

The scientist shook his head. "Not that I know of. The file only concluded it could happen. It didn't say they were doing anything about it." He pulled a treat out of his pocket and broke it in two. Both dogs bounded over.

Sharlene put a cookie on her plate. "I'll contact our team and see if they can look into it." She turned to Max. "Would you mind sharing your data with them?"

"Of course not," the scientist replied. He bent over and pulled his laptop out of his briefcase. "We can't connect this to the internet, though. You never know who might be tracking us online."

Sharlene nodded. "We'll back it up and overnight a thumb drive."

"I'll find a drive." Hank stood and walked to the other side of the room. He began rummaging through the desk by the window.

"Wait. Where's Alex?" Jackie asked, looking around. "I just realized she's missing."

"With all this, I forgot to mention," Sharlene said, clasping her hands. "More bad news." She paused and took a breath. "JT showed up in Sedona. And Alex left with him. He offered her a job she couldn't refuse."

Jackie groaned.

"That's not good," Hank said, returning to the table. He placed a thumb drive in front of Sharlene and took another cookie.

Max also grabbed one and took a big bite. Crumbs fell down the front of his shirt and onto the floor. Fred and George hurried over and cleaned up the mess.

"Why was JT here?" Jackie asked. "And why would Alex go with him?"

"I don't know," Sharlene said. "Alex was upset about something but wouldn't talk to me. She left not long after you did."

"Oh," Zak said. "When we saw Aaron Minor earlier, we took a detour before coming back here, in case they saw us and were following. And Alex ran into her ex."

Jackie gasped. "Finn?"

Zak shook his head. "Another one. Skatter, something like that."

"What happened?" Sharlene asked.

"He showed up at the car while we were pulled over. Freaked her out. She said something about him being her first love and screwing her over."

"Well, whatever it is, there's nothing we can do now." Sharlene sipped her ever-present tea. "She's gone."

"I don't understand what happened," Jackie said. "You're being very calm about this, Sharlene."

Sharlene semi-shrugged. "We can't control other people. I tried to speak with her, but she ran out of the house. I knew she left to drink, so I borrowed a car from the neighbor, so I could find her." Sharlene looked around the table. "By the time I got to her, she'd already signed a contract with JT. And he took her with him."

Sharlene turned to Hank. "I hope you don't mind, but I need you to pick up the spare car from the restaurant."

Hank nodded.

"I'm confused," Dr. Max said. "Who's Alex?"

"I'll tell you later," Jackie replied.

"And are you talking about *the* JT?"

Everyone around the table nodded.

"What does he have to do with this?"

"You don't know?" Sharlene asked.

Dr. Max shook his head.

"He's the one behind all this," Sharlene said. "He owns the lab where you worked. I guess you could say he's your boss."

"He's heading the experiments," Hank added.

"Holy cow," Dr. Max said as his knee knocked into the underside of the table. "I knew I recognized that voice." He glanced around the table at the confused faces. "I never met the funder. It's not unheard of to get research funding from an anonymous source."

Fred and George were still sniffing around Max's legs, hoping to find more cookie treats. Max bent down and picked them up. Once they were securely in his lap, he continued. "When Crystal and Zak escaped, he called me to, let's say, express his displeasure."

"You mean yell at you," Zak said.

Dr. Max shifted uncomfortably. "That's putting it mildly. But I never saw his face. Only heard a voice yelling at me through speakers. And I thought I'd heard it somewhere before. Now I know. It was from TV interviews."

"This doesn't make sense. You don't think Alex...?" Jackie started.

Sharlene shook her head. "No. I think he found her. I'm not sure why he was looking for her, but it's most likely because of Crystal. Bottom line is he offered her a job and a lot of money. And she couldn't say no. Well, didn't want to say no."

"I bet she was drunk," Jackie said.

Sharlene nodded. "Very."

"You don't think she was working with him?" Hank asked.

"No," Sharlene replied. "I'm sure she wasn't. She's simply a lost soul searching for her way. She's not a bad person, just a little misguided."

Jackie's shoulders sagged. "It's my fault. I should have stayed closer to her."

Sharlene reached out and gently patted her wrist. "It's no one's fault, honey. Alex is gonna do what Alex is gonna do." She took her hand away and leaned back. "All of us have to find our own path. And we can't force anyone if they're not ready."

"What now?" Jackie asked.

Sharlene turned to her. "You were right. We have to move. We can't risk staying here any longer."

Jackie stood. "I already found a retreat center where we can stay. I'll go finalize it."

Sharlene nodded. "Alex or JT can't know where we are. I'm sure JT will try to bring her to the dark side."

Hank jumped up. "I'll confirm moving and rearranging the security system." He left the room.

"Next," Sharlene continued, "we need to tell our researchers what the scientist told us." She slid the thumb drive toward the scientist. "If you don't mind making a copy of everything, Dr. Max?"

Dr. Max nodded. "Of course. But, please, call me Max."

Sharlene nodded, a rosy tinge coloring her face.

Dr. Max opened his laptop and turned it on. As he waited for it to boot up, he dug into his backpack and pulled out an instrument they'd never seen before: a black handheld device lined with buttons and flashing lights. It could have come from the set of *Star Trek*.

As the scientist stood, Sharlene stopped him. "Wait a minute. What's that?"

He held it up. "I need some readings from Crystal. If I compare them with the other data, I might be able to figure something out."

Sharlene joined Dr. Max as he walked toward the couch.

He held the device near the side of Crystal's head. Lights flashed as the machine beeped. After nearly a minute, he pulled it away from her. Crystal didn't move or open her eyes as she faded in and out of sight.

The scientist rushed back to his laptop and fed the data into it. He stared at the screen as the information collated and crunched. "Oh" finally escaped his mouth.

"What?" Sharlene asked.

"Um, I'm not one hundred percent sure," Dr. Max replied. "But her energy is fading."

"We know that," Jackie said, returning to the table. "But what can we do?"

"I mean, her quantum energy is fading." The scientist looked at the others, his mushroom cloud hair bouncing. "Energy can't be created or destroyed. It changes and moves, but it always is." He looked back at his computer screen. "But it looks like her energy is starting to actually disappear. It shouldn't be possible."

"This is a catastrophe," Sharlene said. "I'll be right back. I have to call our research team and update them."

Dr. Max continued to crunch numbers and type on his laptop. "Let me try a few things. Maybe a chemical in the gum will help me figure this out."

Sharlene rejoined the group as the scientist disappeared into his work. The tension in the room rose the longer he combed through the data. Time stopped as he stared at the screen and the others made cups of coffee and tea and watched him work.

After several hours and multiple phone calls to Network scientists, Dr. Max pushed back his laptop and sighed. "Okay," he said. "I think we can reverse-engineer a process to put energy back into Crystal and hopefully return her to her dimension."

A collective sigh of relief spread around the table.

The scientist raised his hand. "Don't get too excited. I don't think a modified magnetometer kind of machine will have enough energy to reverse this. We need an energy source."

"What kind of source?" Zak asked.

"I'm not sure. But something magnetic that's an energy conduit."

Sharlene smiled. "You're sitting in the most magnetic place on the planet. Sedona has seven major vortexes."

"Pick the strongest," Dr. Max replied.

"There's only one place," Sharlene said. "Cathedral Rock. It has the most powerful energy around."

Jackie pushed back her chair and stood. "Crystal's getting much worse, so we need to do this now."

Dr. Max rubbed his overly-large nose. "This won't happen tonight. It'll take a couple months or more to modify my equipment and get the exact calibration."

Jackie took a step forward. "We don't have months!"

"I'm sorry," the scientist said, turning back to his computer. "I'll work as fast as I can." He paused and glanced back at them. "I know Crystal is the most important thing to you, but remember, every time JT disconnects a spirit from their energy and the human they're connected to, he puts a little rip in the space-time continuum. Stopping that is our number-one priority." He turned to his screen. "I can't stress that enough. That black hole might suck us all into oblivion."

"Oh, my," Jackie said. "I think I'm in denial about how serious this is."

Dr. Max nodded. "We need to be careful about everything we do. I'm sure I can figure out something to stabilize Crystal for a while. But stopping universal annihilation is top priority."

"Can I get some of the Network team to work with you?" Sharlene asked.

"Most definitely," Dr. Max replied. "I need as many experts and creative thinkers as you can find."

***

As Alex stumbled out of JT's limousine at his Las Vegas casino, she pushed away the uncomfortable feeling gnawing in the pit of her stomach. It was nerves, not the dark-green strands of disgust that colored her hair. JT had arranged an apartment for her on the sixty-second floor of JW, one of his private condo floors, and he had a brand-new Audi waiting in her private parking space. Her signing bonus had been deposited into her bank account.

This was a dream come true. More money than Alex knew what to do with, perks, bonuses, and a job that guaranteed excitement and prestige. This would give her the freedom she'd been looking for. And she was sure her salary would lead her to the kind of husband she wanted.

Three of Five met them in the parking garage and guided Alex to her new apartment. The space was furnished, though she was assured she could change anything. Floor-to-ceiling windows looked out over the Las Vegas Strip and to the desert mountains. The main room was loft style and made the space airy and seem much larger than it was.

The assistant disappeared as Alex wandered to the kitchen. The space boasted top-brand appliances and every home cooking gadget she could think of: espresso machine, mixer, blender, air fryer toaster combo, and small appliances she didn't recognize. She loved how the kitchen and living room were combined, separated by an island big enough to seat four. If only she could cook. She laughed at herself. Forget cooking—she could hire a private chef.

The bedroom was larger than her entire apartment in New Jersey and included a walk-in closet she could actually walk into. There were New York City apartments smaller than her storage space.

The bell rang. Alex headed to the door and found the floor concierge holding two shopping bags.

"Courtesy of JT," the concierge replied as she held out the packages. "He wants you to start tomorrow morning and thought you'd need a few things."

"Thanks." Alex took the bags. She closed the door and brought the packages into the living room, where she sat on the couch and looked at them. Gifts from JT must be part of her job perks. Another reason she belonged there.

Alex reached in and pulled out a Hermes laptop bag, heavy enough that she knew there was a laptop inside. She set it on the cushion next to her and unwrapped the other package. When she saw the Hermes handbag, she gasped.

"It's a Birkin," she said in awe as she held it up to the light. She turned the bag right and left and ran her hands along the buttery leather. Never in her wildest dreams did she think she'd own a top handbag in the world, made by first-class, skilled artisans. It was more beautiful than she could have imagined.

"Holy shit," she said to the room. She was holding at least fifty thousand dollars in her hands. She looked inside and found two iPhones—naturally, the most recent model—as well as her employee ID and a company credit card. The credit card had a note on it that read, "For anything." She put everything back in and closed the bag.

Alex shook her head. "Wow." She placed the Birkin on the coffee table and walked several feet away. She turned and admired it. The bag was so beautiful it made her feel more attractive.

The realization hit her in a flash. This was it. This was the sign she'd been waiting for. She'd finally made it. She was the success she'd always known she could be. Her Birkin represented the happiness she'd finally created for herself.

"Oh, no," Alex said, looking at her jeans and pullover sweater from the backroom used clothing pile in the Sedona house. "These have to go."

She rushed into the bathroom and washed her face, trying to look somewhat presentable. She found deodorant in a drawer and applied the fresh scent. Even the bathroom had come fully stocked.

Alex grabbed her Birkin and headed to the elevator, trying to ignore her growing hangover. She stopped at the concierge desk. The young woman sitting at the station looked like a model; everything about her was perfect: her skin, her clothes, the way she held herself.

"Excuse me. I'm Alex. I didn't get your name when I came in."

The receptionist nodded politely. "I'm Layla. Myself or Ella are here twenty-four hours a day. If you need anything, use the phone by your door." She scribbled a number on a piece of paper and handed it to Alex. "Or call this number."

"Thanks," Alex said, taking the paper and slipping it into her handbag.

She saw Layla's envy as she looked at Alex's new status symbol.

"From JT," Alex said.

"He must think you're special," the concierge replied with a subtle but envious smile.

Alex smiled in return. "Where can I find some appropriate clothes? I've got nothing."

Layla raised an eyebrow ever so slightly but quickly put her professional mask back on. She nodded. "Of course." She pulled out a casino brochure and pointed out the best clothing stores. Nearly every designer of worth had a shop at JW, and more were opening each month as building renovations were completed.

Alex took the private-residence elevator to the main floor. When the doors opened, the sounds of slot machines and voices echoing throughout the cavernous space assaulted her. She made her way to the main casino area and stopped. Alex couldn't believe she was looking at only the first phase of the remodeling and updates. JT had told her on the plane that the casino would double in size within a year. He wasn't building a casino; he was developing a self-contained city within his walls. Guests would never have to leave JW.

Slowly, she looked from left to right, breathing in the overly oxygenated air and the sights around her. For the first time in years, she felt at home. Moreso than even New York City. She didn't realize how much she'd been craving the seductive energy of possibility.

Lights flashed, bells rang, and people slumped at machines as their all-day, all-night gambling binges took them to the brink of exhaustion and bankruptcy.

Alex had never been a fan of Las Vegas—until now. She found it too loud, too flashy, too fake. Too Eurotrash. But after her time in the desert, she was ecstatic to walk through buzzing energy and unbridled opportunity. She meandered through the gold, marble, and red-velvet casino, soaking in the illusion that surrounded her. The sights, sounds, and smells came at her from all directions.

She wandered across the marble floor, past museum-quality modern sculptures and countless tourists. Spotting a store Layla had recommended, she entered to start her shopping spree.

Alex quickly noticed the shop clerks fawning over the other customers, the ones already dressed in designer clothes, while she was ignored as she browsed through the racks. After several minutes of no attention, she headed to the counter. Alex plunked her Birkin down by the register.

"Hi," she said rather curtly to an uninterested attendant. "I start working with JT tomorrow and need help finding clothes I can wear right away."

The shop clerk looked at Alex with indifference. When her eyes drifted to the bag on the counter, she sprang to life.

"Certainly, ma'am," she said with a newfound enthusiasm and charming smile. "Let me show you around."

Alex power-shopped through several stores and bought plenty of clothing and accessories to get her wardrobe started, enough for a couple of weeks. And even though she wasn't a designer size, the clerks found and quickly altered enough for her to feel comfortable. Wealth brought results. And like the elites she'd read about, she had all her purchases sent to her apartment. She wouldn't be seen carting around large shopping bags.

Alex happily charged everything to her company credit card. They were work clothes, after all. Shopping in all the stores she could only dream about before was another tick in her success box.

When she knew she'd collapse if she looked at anything else, she started back to the private-residence elevator. She used her new keycard and called the lift that would take her back to her new life and the thirty thousand dollars' worth of clothes being delivered to her place. She took an excited breath as the soft bell announced the elevator's arrival.

The doors opened. Alex gasped with horror and stepped back. Coming off the elevator mere inches from her was none other than Vinny

DiMachio, former head of Acht Records, where Alex had worked twenty years earlier. He hadn't aged well. He sported dyed-black Elvis hair with what looked like hair plugs on his upper forehead. His skin was gray and sallow, and age spots freckled his face and hands. There was no mistaking that pockmarked face, now cratered with age. It was DiMachio, minus his Jeremy Wickett. The Me Too movement must have driven Jeremy underground—or at least back in his pants.

He walked by Alex without a glance. She stumbled into the elevator, nearly falling over. She teetered as she was thrown back two decades to the trauma of her first job at Acht. Langley and his exploding blood vessels, the abuse she'd suffered at his hands, the dozens of insane interviews that never landed her another job, and Derby's fixation on her. She needed a drink.

Alex forced herself to breathe in slowly. She held her breath for four seconds, then breathed out for seven at the same slow rate. She fought back tears as she ascended to her floor.

Shaking off the nightmare of her past, she inhaled deeply and held up her new bag. Her hand trembled. *It's different this time*, she told herself, looking at her new status symbol and pushing her feelings down. *This time I have the power. I have a Birkin.*

She wiped a teardrop from her eye.

Chapter Ten

Alex woke bright and early for her first day of work. She was a mixture of excited, nervous, anxious, unsure, and confident, just like her first day at college. Her hair wasn't cooperating and flew wildly about her in all shades of a crayon box. Several times after Finn had berated her for having such improbable hair, she'd tried to dye it one color. But her mood colors broke through all the dyes and highlights she tried. Maybe now in Las Vegas—with a new life where she got respect—her hair would be accepted. And so would she.

Knowing first impressions were lasting, she carefully dressed in the Jean Paul Gaultier pinstripe business suit she'd bought the day before. Even though she still carried extra weight from her breakup binge drinking, the suit had been tailored immediately and fit her better than she thought possible. *Expensive clothes do make a person more beautiful*, she thought.

Alex turned from side to side in her full-length mirror. A large, clunky necklace and power boots rounded out her look. She breathed in deeply, promising to get herself a personal trainer and go on a diet next week, after she settled into her new position. In a couple of months, she'd be a force to be reckoned with. In Las Vegas *and* New York City. Nothing would stop her.

She grabbed her power bag, laptop, and other assorted items she thought she might need and headed to her new office. When she entered her executive suite, a stunning young woman in a minidress and legs that didn't seem to end stood up.

"Ms. Scott, I'm Vicky, your executive assistant."

Alex shook her extended hand. She knew the exotic-looking specimen of perfection would be Finn's type. She caught herself and shook off the thought.

"Great to meet you, Vicky. And, please, call me Alex."

Vicky gave a quick nod of acknowledgment. "I have your schedule for today. I also uploaded it onto your calendar."

"Thanks," Alex said, entering her new space. She turned back to her assistant. "Can I get a coffee?"

"Of course. How do you like it?"

"Black is fine." Alex had decided to begin her powerful, new life with small changes, and throwing away the sweetness of cream and sugar was a start. She breathed in. The two leather couches and side chairs had a new-car smell. Her steel-and-glass desk stood in front of large tinted windows overlooking the Strip.

She sat on her desk chair and twirled in circles. Life would be perfect now.

Vicky returned with Alex's coffee and several sheets of paper. She took a seat across from Alex and slid a page toward her.

"You have a meeting with Vinny DiMachio in half an hour."

Alex flinched, last night's wine backwashing into her mouth. Quickly, she swallowed it back down. She'd been hoping the sighting had been a nightmare, but nothing would get in the way this time. Not even a prick like DiMachio. "What's that about?"

"He's the casino's general manager. It's an introductory conversation. He'll fill you in on any ideas for entertainment or events. Or anything they've started planning." Vicky looked up from her copy of the calendar.

"Though I think they've been waiting to fill this position before starting anything."

Alex nodded. A few vodkas were definitely in her evening plans. After DiMachio, she knew she'd need something to wash away her day. "Great. What else?"

Vicky ran through the rest of the scheduled meetings, which included introductory hellos to staff who'd report to her and quick briefings with other department heads.

Alex nodded as she half listened and sipped her bitter coffee. She didn't know how she'd keep everyone and their positions straight.

As if reading her mind, Vicky said, "Don't worry about remembering everyone. My job is to make sure you know who's who."

Alex nodded again. Fuck DiMachio. Fuck her past. This was a new life where she had power. This was her dream job. Even previous assholes from her past wouldn't stop her now.

Half an hour later, Vicky led her to the executive conference room, lounge, and private restaurant on the sixtieth floor.

"I'll leave you here," Vicky said, turning the handle. "This is only for executives."

Alex nodded as her chest expanded and her shoulders straightened. She was one of them. *Finally*.

As Alex entered the massive room, her eyes widened. It was like walking into a private club in New York City. Several conference room–type tables looked like they'd come from a European palace. Comfortable antique couches and chairs decorated the vast lounge, while white-linen-covered restaurant tables took up the far end of the space, close to the windows and view of the Strip. Crystal chandeliers, candles, and museum-quality ornaments had been placed tastefully about the room. Original art hung from the walls. Alex was no connoisseur, but she spotted a Rothko, Picasso, and even a large Jackson Pollock. The room was spacious enough for several meetings to occur at once. It was a private club for the C-Suite elite of the casino.

The executive concierge pointed Alex toward the antique mahogany bar where DiMachio sat in a velvet wingback chair. Two haggard-looking humans were parked on stools on either side.

She took a deep breath and walked confidently to the casino head. She held out her hand. DiMachio remained seated and shook in return, his eyes focused out the window. Alex was shocked at the wet, clammy, limp greeting.

"Mr. DiMachio, I'm Alex Scott. Nice to meet you." Alex sat in a matching wingback chair across from him.

A grunt escaped DiMachio's mouth.

Alex tried again. She looked him in the eye and smiled. "My assistant said this was an introductory meeting since today's my first day. Is there anything you want to know?"

Another grunt.

"Ah, I'm Alpha assistant. I do the talking."

Alex looked to her right at the pale, thin, obviously overworked assistant sitting next to DiMachio and tried to mask her shock. "Excuse me?"

"I speak for Mr. DiMachio. He's very busy."

Alex took in the slimy, pockmarked face of the former music industry king. He kept his eyes focused out the window, avoiding Alex's gaze. DiMachio looked scarred and maimed, like he'd been in combat for decades. And not come out the winner.

Alex looked at Alpha assistant. "That's good to know. Thank you."

Alpha nervously clasped his hands. "Ma'am, look at DiMachio when you speak. I'm just his voice. I'm not him."

Alex felt the clamminess in her armpits. A bead of sweat formed on her forehead. The familiar sick feeling spread across her stomach and up into her throat, but she pushed it away. No one from her past, including DiMachio, would hold her back.

"Sorry, Alpha." She turned to DiMachio. "Would you like to know anything about me?"

"No," Alpha said. "All you need to know is I run this casino. You work for me. If you make me unhappy, you're out the door."

Alex stared at DiMachio, knowing her hair had turned anger black with shades of dark-green disgust. For decades she'd heard that song and dance from insecure executives.

With a nod, she opened her Hermes briefcase. She pulled out a folder and handed it to DiMachio.

"Excuse me," said the other haggard-looking young male on DiMachio's left. "I'm Beta. You hand everything to me."

Alex handed the folder to the other nondescript, nervous-looking assistant and returned her gaze to DiMachio. "I put together some ideas for the department."

Beta took the folder and slid it into his shoulder bag briefcase.

"I don't care what you do," Alpha said. "Bring in any acts, performers, whatever. Have parties. Just make us money. If you don't, you're out."

DiMachio turned to Beta and held out his hand. A newspaper was opened and handed to him. He disappeared behind it.

Alex stood and caught herself from screaming, "Asshole!" She breathed deeply to calm her voice. "Nice to meet you too," she finally said.

She grabbed her Birkin and briefcase and straightened, not bothering to shake DiMachio's hand. She looked at the newspaper blocking her view. "You know, I used to work at Acht Records when you were there."

She took a step toward the door but stopped and glanced back. "And it sucked."

She caught a quick glance of the newspaper being lowered as she turned on her heel. She didn't care. No one would treat Alexandra Marie Scott like shit anymore. Even Vinny fucking DiMachio.

Confidently, Alex walked out of the room, her Birkin swinging by her side.

When she returned to her suite, Vicky stood. "How'd it go?"

Alex shook her head. "Is he that much of an asshole?" she asked as she made her way into her office.

Vicky followed. "Yes."

"How come his assistants were with him?"

"DiMachio got Me Too'ed. I think he has a case against him right now." She placed a pile of folders on Alex's desk. "So he's very cautious. That's why his assistants speak for him and hold everything."

Alex placed her bag on her desk and took a seat. She shook her head. "If that's how everyone is, I don't know…"

"There are some good people here." Vicky pointed to the folders. "These are your other meetings today. I thought you might want some background before you met them."

"After DiMachio, I definitely do." Alex looked at the pile, then at her assistant. "How many meetings do I have today?"

"Twenty."

Alex's jaw dropped. "Twenty? I thought that was a week's worth of meetings earlier. They're all for today?"

Vicky gave her a professional smile. "It's a light day. I think most of your days will be meetings."

Alex leaned back and let out a soft groan. She moved forward in her chair and looked at her assistant. "In the future, let's pass off what we can to people who report to me." She swiveled and glanced out her window. "I'd like to do something creative while I'm here."

"Sure." Vicky pointed to the stack of folders. "These are people who report to you."

"How many people report to me directly?"

"Fifteen. And five of your meetings are with other department heads."

"Great." A bottle of red was sounding good, though drinking was off limits until after six.

Nodding, Alex opened a folder, letting Vicky know the conversation was over. She had to be careful about what she said. Alex had been support staff herself, so she knew how they gossiped among one another. Vicky could be spying for DiMachio. Or JT. She reminded herself she wasn't a friend to any of the employees.

Alex made a note to order some antacids.

***

Day and night, Dr. Max fiddled with the instruments the Spiritual Enterprise Network had sent him. He'd taken over the yoga studio in the back of the wellness retreat center they'd moved to. They'd filled it with a quantum computer, amplifiers, detectors, generators, receivers, chambers, and all sorts of high-tech equipment. He created a makeshift desk from some crates the equipment had come in. He'd even started sleeping on the yoga mats piled in the corner, Fred and George by his side.

In the first couple of days sequestered in his impromptu lab, the scientist developed a subatomic electrical charge that stabilized Crystal. Dozens of Network specialists from all over the world were assisting him. Weak, Crystal spent most of her time lying on the couch or in bed, but her phasing had nearly stopped.

As he worked one morning, the door to the studio opened. He turned and watched as Sharlene, Jackie, Hank, and Zak slipped into the room. Zak sat next to the scientist, as he'd started to do each morning, in case Dr. Max needed anything. Jackie and Hank sat quietly behind him on meditation cushions.

"How's it going?" Sharlene asked, placing tea and granola in front of the scientist. She reached down and pet the two chihuahuas, sneaking them each a treat. They wagged their thanks.

Dr. Max leaned back and gratefully accepted the drink and food. "We've made some progress, but we're not there yet." He leaned forward to look at his computer screen. "I have some data I don't understand, so the team and I need to figure it out."

"Can we help?" Jackie asked.

He shook his head. "I don't think so. At least not right now."

"Can you explain what you're trying to do?" Sharlene asked.

"I don't know how," Dr. Max admitted. "I'm a medical doctor and a research scientist but not a quantum physicist. And we're dealing with quantum entanglement, negative energy, and forces I don't think anyone understands."

"Can you contact some of the physicists who've offered to help you?" Sharlene asked. "I can find more if you want."

"I have a handful helping me now," the scientist said. "I'll check in with them." He looked at the others. "How's Crystal?"

"Better than before," Jackie said. "But not good. She's resting."

"Well, at least she's better than she was." Dr. Max tossed some granola in his mouth and said through his crunching, "I'm gonna get back to work."

They all nodded as he turned back to face his computer.

After phone calls with physicists and many hours of consultations and research, Dr. Max typed up the information he'd jotted down. "Holy cannoli," he said as he raised his arm for emphasis, accidentally hitting his overly large nose.

The others had fallen asleep but woke up and sat at attention. "What? You okay? What's up?" Hank, Jackie, and Zak said in unison.

"Sorry. Pardon my language," he said distractedly, looking from one document to the other, his mushroom cloud hair bouncing.

"What's going on?" Jackie asked.

Sharlene walked in with sandwiches as Jackie spoke. "What's happening?"

Dr. Max looked at the Network head. "Have a seat. I think we have something."

Sharlene pulled up a crate and sat next to him. She passed around the plate of wraps and vegan sandwiches. "What's up?"

The scientist shook his head. "The team of people you connected me with has a pretty plausible theory." He looked at them all seriously. "Remember, this is a theory, and it could take years to prove, if at all. We think the spirits are materializing near the human they were guiding. And we think your friend Alex was energetically connected to Crystal. That's why Crystal appeared near her and why they found each other."

"How did they figure that out?" Sharlene asked.

"I don't know how to explain it," the scientist said. "But the calculations and data seem to point in that direction."

"What does that have to do with Crystal?" Hank asked.

"It's part of the puzzle," Dr. Max said. "There's more. Remember how the secret researcher at my old lab reported that the people who were disconnected to spirits might also eventually die?" Everyone nodded. "Well, they aren't dropping dead on the street or vanishing into thin air.

They most likely deteriorate slowly, so severing the energetic connection could mean they're losing the will to live."

"Wow," Jackie said. "We don't know Alex that well, but she's been going downhill since I met her. Her drinking was getting out of control."

Dr. Max nodded. "Yes. The disconnected people might be committing suicide, overdosing, engaging in risky sexual behaviors, or drinking themselves to death. They could also be extremely violent and not care if they kill or are killed. That kind of thing."

"Interesting hypothesis," Sharlene said. "I'll see if I can find any statistics for those behaviors. Maybe that could give us some kind of clue and eventually help with something."

"Great idea," Dr. Max said. "Thanks."

"I still don't understand why this is important," Hank said.

"One step at a time, my friend," the scientist said. "I don't either, but it's a clue."

He turned back to his machine and took a big bite of his hummus wrap.

***

By week two, Alex had fallen into a routine. Breakfast meetings, a quick run to her office to check in with Vicky and go over the day's agenda, more meetings, lunch meetings, afternoon meetings, dinner meetings or a show, and emails at night to follow up on the meetings.

After a month, Alex felt like she'd been in her Las Vegas job for years. She had work friends, colleagues, and a new life adventure unfolding in front of her. It was everything she'd always dreamed of. DiMachio had been true to his word and left her alone. She was in charge, not dominated by ex-boyfriends like Finn or former bosses like Langley, or under anyone's day-to-day control. She was an executive vice president, after all.

Alex had a staff of fifty, so people reported to people who reported to people, and only the people at the top reported to her. She didn't have to hire or fire—or do any grunt work. She got to do what she loved: develop and organize creative events and experiential marketing campaigns for the casino. If she mentioned something, people brought the concept to life. Even the endless meetings didn't bother her; she was in charge, so the staff had to listen to her. She had the power to create—and destroy—ideas and people's careers, which she found intoxicating.

Days blended together. In no time, she had bills from New York paid off and a large sum of money in the bank. She lived at the casino rent free, so there was no point in moving and paying rent or a mortgage. She expensed most of her meals, and her entertainment was covered. The rich did get richer.

Alex was content enough. Whenever the now-familiar nagging feeling chewed at her stomach, she found some wine or snacks to calm herself down. She was definitely living a successful life, one most people could only dream of.

She arrived in her office after her third breakfast meeting. When she looked at her calendar, she smiled with delight. Her old friend, Hellie, from her record company days, was scheduled for lunch.

Alex breezed through her morning, reprimanding four subordinates and eating only one roll of antacids. Before she knew it, she was walking into the Michelin-starred dining area in the private executive meeting room one of the top floors of the casino. Only vice presidents and above could eat at Jackson's, the most exclusive restaurant in Las Vegas. This was one of the perks of her job that Alex loved.

She spotted Hellie across the room. She might have aged twenty years, but she still had her Midwest innocent glow. And she didn't look any older. Or perhaps they were aging at the same rate, so Alex didn't notice.

As Alex neared the table, she opened her arms and squealed. Hellie jumped up, her mousey brown hair still limp and falling into her face like it did twenty years earlier. They hugged each other tightly.

"I can't believe it's you," Alex said as she released Hellie. An invisible waiter held Alex's seat for her. She sat down and looked at her friend. Hellie had been the unassuming, petite, pale receptionist on the executive floor at Acht Records, just down the hall from Alex. She wasn't ugly; she was simply so ordinary people didn't notice her. Hellie's averageness allowed her to hide in plain sight; Alex had always felt sorry for her.

Hellie had never complained about the yelling or the abusive treatment the support staff had suffered at Acht. Instead, she'd spent her days answering phones and tapping her Ticonderoga number two pencil against the glass of the aquarium she'd kept on her desk. Mutant sea creatures swam happily inside as Hellie painstakingly trained them to dance to her favorite music.

Menus were placed in front of them.

Alex opened hers and glanced at the day's specials. She had the rest of the menu memorized. "Let's do this before we talk."

The two gave their orders to the waiter, who was invisible except for the pen and pad floating in the air.

"Anything to drink?" glided toward them.

Alex turned to Hellie. "What do you think? Some wine?"

Hellie shook her head. "Sorry. I gave it up years ago."

"Gave up what?"

Hellie smiled. "Drinking."

Alex leaned back, trying to mask her shock. "You didn't."

Hellie nodded. "Two kids, a husband, two rescue dogs, and a full-time career. Oh, and perimenopause. A couple drinks and I'd have a hangover for two or three days. Something had to go."

The knife of jealousy dug into Alex's gut. "You have kids? And a husband?"

Hellie glowed. "I have a beautiful family I'm super proud of."

Alex forced a smile. She reached out and touched her wineglass, nodding toward a hovering pad and pen. "That's so amazing. Congratulations."

Hellie leaned forward. "What about you? Are you and Skeater still together?"

Alex let out a sarcastic laugh. "No. We broke up years ago. Fame and monogamy didn't mix well with him."

Hellie reached her hand across the tablecloth. "I'm sorry."

Alex pulled her hand away before Hellie could touch her. "Don't be. Getting away from him was the best thing I've ever done." She paused for a second, thinking. "Well, after getting out of that hellhole called Acht."

They both laughed.

Alex's usual pinot grigio was placed in front of her. She ignored Hellie's raised eyebrow as she took a long sip. It was six o'clock somewhere. And she needed a drink. Plain Jane Hellie had a husband and kids. Alex had assholes and abuse. Her hair streaked envy chartreuse.

Alex put down her glass. "How are things going? You're headlining at the Bellagio, I see."

Hellie's face lit up. "Can you believe it? Those mutant sea creatures from our days at the record company. I never thought they'd be my career."

"Crazy. You're so lucky." Alex took another sip of her wine, trying to numb the nagging feeling in her gut. She might need to cancel her meetings that afternoon because this called for at least two glasses of wine, perhaps a bottle.

Lunch was served. Alex dug into her Cobb salad. "Have you kept in touch with anyone?" She put a forkful of avocado and ham into her mouth.

Hellie shook her head. "Not really. I've heard some gossip, though."

"Like what?" Alex said, chewing her food.

Hellie paused for a second. "Oh, remember Zena?"

Alex swallowed and nodded.

"Triplets."

"What the F?"

Hellie nodded. "I know. She married her boss in promotion, Jiglio, and had triplets. From what I know, she's fat and happy in North Jersey somewhere."

Alex reached for her wine and took another long sip. Even fellow assistant and brainless Zena got married and had kids. Her lingerie-looking wardrobe had obviously paid off.

"And Weena?" Hellie continued. "The one who always had body parts falling off and had to constantly glue them back on?"

Alex nodded. The media executive was always so stressed out and panicked that pieces of her body would randomly fall off all the time. Alex would jump out the window if Weena had triplets.

"She took a yoga course and now goes around wearing a turban and tells everyone she's enlightened."

"Seriously?"

Hellie nodded. "A couple of years ago, she even came to my office, asking me for a job. Pre-turban."

Alex shook her head. "What about my old boss, Langley? What's he up to?"

Hellie lit up as she leaned forward. "You'll like this. He blew so many blood vessels in his neck that they had to graft in silicone. The blood couldn't get out, so if he gets angry now, he shoots blood from his mouth, nose, ears, and even eyes!"

"Is he still in music?"

Hellie shook her head. "I think he left ages ago. He married the assistant who replaced you and had a couple kids. Then he got fired, but I don't know why."

Even her sadistic, nasty, abusive former boss had gotten married and created a family. Alex held up her glass, which was immediately refilled. She took another long sip and did her best to make everything look okay, even though streaks of anger black highlighted her hair and mixed with the yellow-green of envy.

Alex put down her wine. "What's he doing?"

Hellie laughed. "He ended up as an ambulance chaser in Albuquerque. Apparently, his face is plastered on billboards all over the state."

Alex snorted. "Well, it's a step up from the lawyer he was."

Hellie nodded.

After their meal, Alex sat back with her fourth glass of wine. She pulled out her phone and texted Vicky, telling her to cancel her meetings and have her laptop dropped off at her apartment. Alex could work from there for the rest of the day. Or pass out. Drinking until she passed out was looking like the better option.

Alex folded her napkin and placed it on the table. She leaned back, concentrating so she could enunciate her words. "Are you under contract at the Bellagio?"

Hellie nodded and put down her cup of tea. "For five more years. The shows sell out up to six months in advance."

"For real?"

Hellie nodded, a slight blush coloring her cheeks. "I know. It's been such a fun, crazy ride. Who would have thought I'd be here?"

Alex certainly wouldn't have believed it. She caught herself and pushed the thought away. No need to be a bitch. She was happy for Hellie—that's what she told herself, even though the sick feeling in her stomach said otherwise. She glanced at her Birkin on the small stand they'd placed next to her chair when she arrived. She reminded herself she was successful and living her dream life. Alex silently repeated her mantra several more times.

"I guess that means I can't convince you to perform here?"

Hellie shook her head. "Thank you so much for asking. I'm really flattered, but I'm not leaving." She folded her napkin and placed it on the table. "I'm happy there."

"I could offer you double what you get now."

"Again, thank you. But I don't need more money. Things couldn't be any better. I really am living the life of my dreams."

Alex sipped her wine in disbelief. How could anyone turn down the kind of money she was offering Hellie. She definitely needed a vodka when she got back to her apartment. She brushed away Hellie's words. "I control all the events here at the casino, so I wanted to ask."

Hellie pushed back her chair. "Thanks again, but I have to get back. The SeaCreats, as I call them, are learning a new routine, so I have to train them."

Alex nodded, not bothering to get up.

Hellie briefly put her hand on Alex's shoulder. "Stay in touch. It was wonderful to see you."

Alex nodded again, unable to squirm away from Hellie's hand. Everyone she knew had a family and was happy, even plain Hellie and brainless Zena. And she was still alone.

Hellie leaned down. "Alex, there's more to life than work."

Alex snorted. "No, there's not." She looked at Hellie. "At least not for me." She sat back. Sour stabs of pain whirlpooled in her stomach.

Hellie gave her a warm pat. "I'm just down the road. Call me if you need anything." She started to leave then stopped. She leaned back toward Alex. "And don't take the whole menopause thing lightly. It can wreak havoc."

Alex waved Hellie off and spoke to her near-empty glass of wine. "Oh, seriously, I'm too young for any of that. And things couldn't be more perfect. The money, the responsibility, the things I do. My life couldn't get any better."

She watched her former colleague, now an internationally successful entertainer trainer, as she walked lightly from the restaurant. She then looked at her Birkin, but it didn't bring comfort this time.

Alex stood up and steadied herself against the table. Maybe firing a few staff members would help.

Chapter Eleven

JT paced the length of his palatial Manhattan headquarters office, guzzling antacids and sucking on his processed protein drink. He was eating so many tablets now he carried two or three stormtrooper dispensers. He'd found it annoying at first, but once he started playing war games with them, he quite enjoyed the company.

For more than a month, Alex had been under all types of surveillance, but she wasn't connecting with the Sedona group. As much as JT got off watching her, something had to be done. Alex was his ticket inside the group and to more money. JT thought it would take a couple of days, but she was taking forever. His security team couldn't crack their computer systems, and his satellites had been equally as useless. JT needed her to lead him in so he could sabotage their plans and steal anything they might have created.

JT had been building Alex up, but once she got him access to the Network, he would slowly bring her to her knees. He wanted to control and crush her bit by bit. The thought made him hard.

"One," JT screamed into his intercom. "Get in here. *Now*."

The door opened before JT had time to shut off his speaker. A stone-faced One of Five entered.

"There's been nothing about Alex?"

One shook his head. "No, sir. No communication with them at all."

"Fuck." JT turned his back to his assistant and continued to pace. "Get the hell out of here!" he screamed as he stormed across the room.

After breaking his lightsaber on the ficus tree, JT had paused his swashbuckling. The store-bought swords he'd tried broke within a day. And his *Star Wars* weapon had been an actual prop used on the movie set. Getting it fixed would take months.

JT's anger grew as each day passed. With his venting explosions reaching an all-time high, he was having himself changed at least twice a day. Without his sword, he needed another way to relieve his stress.

The billionaire wandered to his desk and turned on his surveillance monitors in Las Vegas. He was tracking Alex in her apartment, office, and other places in between. JT watched her jumping from phone call to meeting to video call, racing back and forth from her office to just about everywhere in the casino. But no contact with Crystal and no information about what they were doing. All she did was work.

JT let out a deep-throated scream as he stared at the monitor. "What the fuck is wrong with you, bitch? Just fucking call them. It's not that hard."

He watched as Alex stumbled into her apartment. She staggered to her kitchen and grabbed a glass and the bottle of vodka on the counter.

JT looked at his watch. It was 2:00 p.m. in Las Vegas, and she was already drunk. He shook his head as she staggered to the couch and fell onto it. He zoomed in closer and felt the tingling in his groin as he watched her sip her drink, defeat oozing from her pores.

A smile slowly crept its way across his face. His next conquest was primed and ready for him.

JT hit his intercom. "One. We're going to Vegas. *Now*."

***

The cool tile of the bathroom floor comforted Alex. She wiped her mouth with her washcloth. She'd spent most of the night drinking, crying, and throwing up. Revisiting her past hadn't been smart, so Hellie was off her friend list. If she didn't see something, there was less of a chance she'd think about it.

The room spun as she stumbled from the bathroom and collapsed onto her bed. She picked up her phone and texted Vicky, letting her know she'd be working from her apartment. Alex also asked her to cancel all meetings that day; her excuse being that she was fighting the flu.

Vicky responded almost immediately, confirming she had canceled all meetings. Except one. Alex was scheduled to have early-evening drinks with JT.

Alex groaned and rolled over. *Fuck.* JT didn't take no for an answer. She turned and vomited the last of her stomach into the trash can next to her bed.

She woke hours later. The sun streamed through her window, so it had to be late afternoon. She glanced at her clock. Four. Her meeting with JT was at six.

Fuck, fuck, fuck, fuck. Alex slowly got off her bed. She stumbled to the kitchen and grabbed a couple bottles of Vitamin Water and her supersized bottle of Advil. She downed three tablets with the sugar water and slowly got herself ready for her meeting. Her entire body felt heavy and disconnected, and her brain was cloudy with hangover haze.

Alex showered, brushed her teeth, and tried to get her wildly improbable ill shaded, lime-green-streaked hair in some kind of shape. She looked at herself in the mirror. Dark circles were painted under her eyes, and her skin appeared gray and sallow. She took a deep breath and closed her eyes.

She told herself she was fine. It was only a hangover.

She made her way to JT's casino office. He wasn't in Las Vegas often, so when he showed up in person, Alex knew she had to be ready for him anytime, for anything.

One of Five showed her into the global kingpin's palatial suite and pointed to the other side of the room. The space was bigger than many homes. When Alex walked over to JT and his view of the Strip, he held out an extremely full glass of vodka, with three small ice cubes tinkling around the crystal.

Her stomach turned at the sight of more alcohol. Alex took the glass and stood next to him. "Nice to see you, JT."

"Of course," was his reply. JT flipped open his stormtrooper dispenser and popped a few tabs into his mouth. He moved to his black leather couch, sat down, and patted the cushion next to him. "Have a seat. How work's going?"

Alex's insides screamed for her to get out. Her hair streaked fear maroon and anxious red. But she knew where her bread was buttered, so she obligingly walked over and sat on the couch next to him. JT gently lifted the vodka glass toward Alex's mouth. She sipped.

After a few mouthfuls, Alex's body relaxed. The screaming voice was silenced. Her hangover disappeared. Alcohol was the cure for her drinking.

"I want an update on your department," JT said, staring at her from head to toe, lingering on her chest. He lifted his drink from the coffee table and took a sip. He put the cold, wet glass against Alex's inner thigh as he bent to put it back on the table.

Alex was disgusted yet eerily turned on. "Things are going great. We have six different shows in the works. The first two are on sale."

She ignored JT's hand on her knee. She was getting wet as he slowly rubbed it up and down her leg. "Um," she said, distracted. "One show sold out. Um. For three months."

"You're doing a great job, Alex," JT murmured in her ear as his hand parted her legs. "I want you to keep it up." He took his other hand and tipped her glass to her mouth.

Alex swallowed a large mouthful of vodka. She froze and disappeared in her head to her safe space. With both hands, JT spread her legs even wider. He put his hands inside her stretch crepe pants and shoved his fingers inside her. She tried to finish her vodka but cried out from the pain.

Alex heard the "pffffts pffffts pffffts" as JT pulled off her pants. She came back to the room as she gagged from the smell. But it was too late. He knocked the glass out of her hand and pinned her on the couch. He panted heavily and leaned toward her. "This is part of your job," he said gruffly through his grunting. He bit her ear.

She cried out as she lost herself in an alcoholic haze of dissociation. A small voice screamed for her to fight and get out. But another voice told her she deserved it. She needed to be humiliated. It was what she knew.

Alex gave up. She didn't care. She hated herself.

JT pushed harder inside her.

Alex couldn't focus. She was a spectator, watching someone else. Everything was happening outside her. Her clothes were on the floor. JT was on top of her, grinding his stomach and hips into her. He fumbled to pull down his zipper. He threw himself on her and crushed his body against hers as he shoved himself into her. Even though he was small and flaccid, he thrust away.

Alex's head slammed into the arm of the couch as JT ground into her. Even through her alcohol-fueled, dissociative haze, she felt his frustration build. His thrusting wasn't to please her; it was to help him get hard. But all he could do was limply hump her. She felt his flabby penis fall out.

He grabbed her neck and pressed down hard, choking her. Alex fought to breathe as she coughed out short, ugly gasps in a mixture of pain and disgusted pleasure. She climaxed as a tear rolled down her cheek.

She felt the weight of JT's body roll off her and heard him finish himself off. She swallowed her sobs and kept her eyes closed as he zipped up his pants.

JT's fart-encrusted breath blew into her ear. "You're here for whatever I need, whenever I need it, you slut. *Anything* I need."

Alex felt the sting of the hard, backhanded fist on her face before she understood what had happened.

She kept her eyes closed as he moved away.

"It'll be even better next time," JT said, walking away. He stopped and turned around. "And there *will* be a next time."

Alex curled into the fetal position, covering as much of her body as she could. As soon as she felt silence in the room, she broke down and sobbed. Her hair turned a mixture of every sad and defeated shade in her mood color wheel. After some time, she opened her eyes and dressed herself, making sure not to look at her body.

She groaned as she stood up. She wiped her eyes and blew her nose. The room spun as she straightened. Alex grabbed the couch and threw up on the velvet cushions. She felt the pain between her legs as she tried to walk. Her face and eye stung.

She hated him. She hated herself. She hated the world. Alex grabbed her laptop and bag and staggered across JT's office, realizing she was reliving Finn and her childhood all over again. She choked back a sob.

As Alex made her way out of the office, she glanced briefly at JT's three Las Vegas assistants. They were frozen behind their computers, not daring a glance in her direction. Her body somehow made it to the elevator as she floated outside herself.

Alex stumbled into her apartment and collapsed on her couch. She was numb inside and out. She floated in nothingness as she threw up all over herself.

A few minutes later, she closed her eyes and fell into the dark relief of unconsciousness.

***

For the next week, Alex canceled all meetings and worked from her apartment. Or at least she told her assistant she was working when she wasn't fighting her made-up flu. The black eye wasn't too obvious, but she couldn't face anyone. Her own self-disgust was more than she could handle. Her hair remained a rainbow of despair.

She wanted to fall asleep and never wake up. JT's humiliation was bad enough, but believing she deserved the pain disgusted her to her core. She was the freak she'd always feared.

Alex had put up with Finn's violent sex games because he'd told her that was love and trust. Like a fool, she'd believed him. She'd put up with Skeater's constant screwing around and lying. Even though he didn't physically hurt her, she still suffered.

Alex never knew otherwise. To her, pain was being a woman. To love meant to suffer. She'd learned that from her brother, who'd forced her to say how much she liked the way he hurt her. And from her father, who'd insisted his punishment was for her own good.

She'd always been too ashamed to talk about it, even with her therapist.

But JT. This was so much worse. The pain and humiliation of the past should have disappeared once she landed her dream job at the casino. But it had followed her. Again.

Her jobs, from Acht Records, to Klein Strategies, to the casino, and other short-term jobs in between, were riddled with abuse. Her relationships were violent and violating. She didn't have any real friends. She must have done something horrifically wrong in a past life. It was all her fault.

The following days were a blur of alcohol, tears, hangovers, and what little work Alex could do. She couldn't think, nor could she shake her dissociated state and come back into her body. Alex comforted herself with bottles of white wine during the day and red at night. She couldn't look at vodka anymore. Thinking about the smell made her gag.

A week following her attack, Alex was on her couch, a bottle of white already gone. Crystal popped into her head for the umpteenth time. She wondered how she was and if Jackie and Sharlene had returned her to her dimension. She surprised herself when she realized she missed them. Tears filled her eyes.

Alex stared at her personal Sedona phone sitting on the coffee table. She'd put it there days ago. She couldn't find her burner but knew she'd somehow synced Jackie's number with this phone while settling into her Las Vegas life. Alex wanted to contact Jackie but couldn't. Her hair was streaked shame salmon and her stomach felt like it was eating itself from the inside out. She leaned over, grabbed the trash can, and vomited her wine into the bin.

She grabbed a tissue and wiped her mouth. A tear rolled down her cheek.

They would hate her; she knew it. They wouldn't speak to her.

Alex threw up again. She sat back and grabbed the glass of red wine from the coffee table. She took a drink, swishing the wine around her mouth to get rid of any remaining vomit.

She swallowed and grabbed the phone; she was seeing double. She closed one eye and opened up her text messages. She found Jackie's number and clumsily typed, *Hi. It's Alex. Sorry. Had to go. F'ed up. How u?*

Alex hesitated, then hit "send," tears rolling down her face. A few minutes later, she passed out.

***

JT's intercom buzzed.

"Sir, she messaged one of them."

"Fucking finally," JT said. "What did you find out?"

"Nothing yet, sir. She just sent a text. No reply yet."

"Keep me posted." JT clicked off the intercom in his New York office and sat back. He sipped his ever-present processed protein drink and pulled out a packet of genetically modified potato chips. Alex had actually turned out to be an excellent employee, probably one of the best he'd ever hired. And she liked it rough. She wanted to be punished. JT let out a satisfied "phrfffffft" as his dick tingled.

But he needed the information from her, and he would make her give it to him. Slapping her around was a pleasant perk. He shoved a large handful of chips into his mouth and crunched loudly as crumbs spilled down his shirt and onto his desk.

***

Weeks passed as Dr. Max researched, studied, and drew up designs with a group of physicists and designers from the Network.

One morning, everyone was in the yoga studio lab in their usual positions. Sharlene handed out tea and biscuits while Hank and Jackie sat on meditation cushions and watched the scientist work. Jackie puffed vigorously on her unlit American Spirit. Hank sat motionless, as he did most days. Crystal had started joining them and lay on a pile of yoga mats and blankets.

Zak sat beside the scientist, reading through the data the team was compiling. Fred and George were visiting everyone in the room one by one in the hopes of a treat.

Sharlene sat on a cushion. "The Network research team contacted us this morning." She nodded toward Dr. Max. "They've been researching statistics on suicide rates, deaths, that sort of thing."

"What did they find?" Jackie asked.

"They said they can't prove a specific link, but they found a significant uptick in everything, from suicide to alcoholism to road rage, over the past two years."

"So Max was right," Jackie said.

"The Network can't officially say that, but it sounds like it to me," said Sharlene.

Dr. Max had his back to the room as he furiously typed on his computer, his mushroom cloud hair bouncing to the tune of his typing. He banged the keys, made notes on his pad of paper, and suddenly sat back.

"Yes!" he yelled, thrusting his arms in the air.

"What?" rang around the room.

The scientist turned on his printer and produced a set of schematics. He showed the paper to the room. "We have a machine!"

"Great! Yeah! Wonderful!" echoed around the room.

"What does that mean, though?" Jackie asked.

Dr. Max spun around in circles in his chair. He stopped and looked at them. "It's the Crystalizer." He pointed to the paper and looked at Crystal. "I named it after you."

Crystal smiled. "That's so nice of you. Thanks."

Dr. Max laughed. "Least I could do." He looked back at the room. "Okay, we have no time to waste. Your team said they'll overnight anything we don't have here, but let's start building this thing."

"What's it for, though?" Sharlene asked.

"If our calculations are correct," the scientist said, "it'll reverse the process Crystal went through, and send her back where she belongs. And stop the mini black holes from ripping apart space-time."

A round of applause erupted throughout the room.

"Okay," Dr. Max said. "Let's start with the quantum computer. It's the heart of the machine. Then we'll add everything else around it."

The room jumped to life as everyone cleared space and started building the machine that hopefully would save Crystal—and the universe.

***

Jackie spent two days in the lab helping Dr. Max. On day three, she showered. As she headed downstairs to continue her work, she grabbed her phone from her nightstand. She hadn't looked at it since she'd started building the Crystalizer. When she looked at the screen, she gasped. She raced to the kitchen, where Sharlene was making lunch.

"You won't believe this," Jackie said, bursting into the room.

"What is it?" Sharlene asked.

Jackie sat at the table. "Alex messaged."

"Oh, my, about time." Sharlene wiped her hands on a tea towel and joined Jackie at the table.

Jackie opened the text. "She says she's sorry for leaving. Asked how we're doing. Said things are fucked up." She looked across the table. "What do you think? Should I answer her?"

Sharlene nodded slowly. "We should be careful, but yes, let's hear what she has to say. And see how she's doing. She doesn't sound good."

"What should I tell her about Crystal?"

"Be truthful, but just give the minimum."

Jackie picked up her phone and texted back, All good. Crystal okay. Not 100%. We think we have solution. Why didn't u speak 2 us b4 going?

She read it quickly to Sharlene, got her approval, and hit "send."

***

When Alex came to, she checked her phone. Nothing. She leaned over and threw up what little she had left in her stomach. She dropped her cell onto the coffee table and leaned back.

They hated her. Everyone hated her. She had nothing. Why was she alive? Alex had no real friends, no purpose, no reason to live. She grabbed the wine bottle and drank until she passed out again.

For two days, she continued drinking, checking her phone, throwing up, and crying until she passed out.

On the third day, Alex woke up, her back aching from sleeping on the couch. She sat up and swung her legs to the floor, still drunk. She panted to catch her breath, her heart pounding furiously in her chest. What was the point?

She looked around her apartment. Wine and vodka bottles littered the room, along with room service and takeout containers. She was back in New Jersey, only with a better view.

Alex picked up her phone, like the dozens of times she had over the past few days. She opened it and gasped. Jackie had texted back.

Alex threw up in the trash. She stared at the notification, terrified to open the message. When she finally got the nerve to click into the text, she cried.

A text exchange started, with Alex explaining she thought they were angry because she left to work for JT. That she couldn't turn her dream job down. Jackie replied that they wouldn't have held her back and wished her well. Her last message asked if Alex still had her other phone.

Alex stumbled into her bedroom. The burner had to be around the boxes and bins stuffed with apartment things she'd bought and hadn't gotten around to using. It was the only place left. She reached into the back of her walk-in closet and under her hanging clothes. She rummaged through piles of kitchen appliances, cooking gadgets, and an assortment of household goods. Now that she had money, she was buying unnecessary things simply because she wanted to. It helped her feel better for a while.

There were boxes thrown into bins and miscellaneous items strewn around. She dropped onto the closet floor and felt around until she found the burner. Alex also found the charger and plugged her cell into the outlet in the closet. She closed her eyes and rolled onto her back.

She jumped when the phone rang. She nervously hit the "answer" button. Her heart pounded. She willed herself not to throw up. "Hello?"

"Hey."

Alex didn't realize how much she'd missed Jackie until she heard her voice.

"How's it going?" Alex slurred, tears filling her eyes.

"Well, now that I know you're okay, I'm fine."

"Thanks." Alex wiped away some snot that had dripped from her nose.

"You are okay, yes?" Jackie asked.

Alex hesitated for several seconds, then said through tears, "Yes. I'm good."

"Alex, what's wrong?"

The kindness in Jackie's voice broke her. She sobbed into the phone, unable to speak.

"Alex, whatever it is, you can come back. You're always welcome here."

"No, no, I can't," Alex choked out. "I'm a horrible person."

Nothing else would come out.

"Alex, come back. Or I'll come get you. You need to get out of there."

Alex sobbed, her tears flowing as she noisily cried. "I can't," she managed. She heaved and vomited wine all over her rug.

"Alex, listen to me. There's a reason you found Crystal. You two are connected. She was your guiding spirit. Things have been falling apart because JT separated her from you. This isn't your fault."

"It's all my fault," Alex sobbed.

"We're taking Crystal to Cathedral Rock early tomorrow morning. We think we've figured out how to get her back. Come say goodbye. It'll help. And I know she'll want to see you."

Alex couldn't speak through her sobbing.

"Please come," Jackie said.

Alex ended the call and hurled her phone across the room. Loud choking sobs filled her apartment as she crawled out of her closet and crumpled into a ball. She cried until she passed out.

Chapter Twelve

JT looked up as One popped his head into the office.

"She made contact."

JT stood up. "What happened? Am I getting a copy?"

"Copy was just sent."

JT started pacing. "Give me the CliffsNotes."

One of Five stepped into the office and closed the door. "Apologies back and forth. Crystal's still alive. The other person asked if Alex had her phone. And that was it."

"Phone. What phone?" JT asked. "I thought we took or bugged everything of hers."

"Not sure, sir."

"Well, fucking find out."

JT pffft'ed and turned his back on his assistant. *Fucking morons*, he thought. When he turned back, One was gone. JT needed another way to get Alex to talk. And he needed a fix.

He walked to his desk and pressed his intercom.

"Yes, sir," One of Five barked through the speaker, as he'd been instructed.

"Make a dinner reservation for two at my steakhouse in Vegas for seven tonight. Make sure I have a private room. Tell Alex Scott she's my guest. Don't give a reason. And get me to the plane now."

***

When Alex learned JT had booked her for dinner that night, a mixture of terror and humiliation coursed through her. Not only would he fire her, but she also knew he would destroy her.

Alex spent the rest of the day vomiting and trying to calm herself. She knew she should run from JT, but she couldn't. Paralyzed, she hated herself even more for not being strong enough to leave.

At seven o'clock, she made her way to the casino floor and W Steaks. When she was ushered into an empty private room, her stomach sank. He was firing her. He didn't want her around after what he'd done to her.

Alex sat at the only table. A glass of red wine appeared in front of her. She saw what looked like two or more bottles of wine in the decanter. Well, at least they would drink. If she blacked out, she wouldn't know what happened.

JT arrived his usual half hour late, on time by his standards. Alex hastily stood, feeling the two glasses of wine she'd already had. She shook his extended hand and wrapped herself in denial. When he squeezed her palm hard, then violently pinched her finger, she blushed. She sat down, catching her breath. Dark-green strands of disgust sprinkled throughout her hair, along with fear maroon and dreaded purple excitement.

He had her wineglass refilled while a glass of vodka was placed before him. He took a sip and put his glass down. "I thought we should have a casual check-in. How are things?"

Alex tried to quell the uneasiness growing in her stomach. "Um. Things are good. If I'd known you wanted a report, I would have written something up." She looked at his vodka then the decanter of wine next to them. Did he expect her to drink all that?

JT smiled. "No, no. I don't care about the business. I get all those reports. You're doing much better than I thought anyone could." He leaned toward her. "I mean, how are you settling in? Do you miss being slapped?"

Alex reeled. He was so open about it, so nonchalant about wanting to hurt her. A soft throbbing spread between her legs. She took a large mouthful of wine.

"Oh." She fake smiled and gestured to the room, pushing down the truth trying to get out. "How can I not be happy? Look at all this. I mean, this is a dream come true. This is where I belong."

JT held up his glass. "Then let's toast you and your success."

The two clinked glasses and drank.

With another ugly grin, JT held up his glass again. "And to me forcing you into submission."

Alex drank deeply, pretending not to hear.

Casual conversation peppered the meal as they ate and drank. Alex relaxed as JT kept the conversation light and the wine loosened her up. He was acting like a gentleman. She must have overreacted to everything before.

When Alex stood to go to the restroom, the alcohol hit. She steadied herself with the back of the chair as the room tilted.

"You okay?" JT asked.

She knew the question was insincere; he was trying to get her drunk. Carefully, she made her way to the restroom. She zigged and zagged across the tile floor and banged her head against the bathroom stall as she tried to lock the door.

After relieving herself, Alex looked in the mirror in horror. Her hair was a combination of shocking white, fear maroon, and anxious red, peppered with dark-green strands of disgust. She had raccoon eyes, the look drunk women get when their mascara and eyeliner smear around their eyes. She redid her makeup as best she could and staggered back to the table.

She knew she was past the point of no return, but it didn't matter. She knew what was coming, so she'd rather be blackout drunk than remember what he did to her.

Alex reached the table and grabbed the back of the seat. She lowered herself onto the cushion but caught the edge of the chair. She lost her balance and fell bottom first onto the floor, landing with a thud, unsure where she was or what was happening.

JT loomed over her, his hand outstretched and a grin on his face. Clumsily, Alex raised her arm and was helped into her seat.

"Whoops," he said. "Gotta watch those chairs. They can be dangerous."

Alex shook her head from side to side, words failing her. She glanced at the glass in front of her and groaned. It was nearly full. Again.

"Let's celebrate you," JT said. "Before I tie you up and choke you."

She shook her head, her eyes glued to the glass that never emptied. She was reliving her childhood nightmares.

"The wine is five hundred a bottle, so I figure you need to finish it." JT toasted her with his nearly empty glass of vodka. "Before you're mine." His eyes bored into her. "And you're going to like it."

Alex half heard his words and tried to ignore him. Unable to speak, she picked up her glass and waved it in his general direction. Wine sloshed onto the tablecloth and her head bobbed sloppily.

"Have you met many people since coming here?" JT asked.

Alex took a sip of wine and closed her eyes, the realization overwhelming her: alcohol was her only friend. She put down her glass and did her best to form the words to answer him. "I have work friends."

"You don't see your friends from before?"

Alex heard JT, but he was down a long tunnel, far away from her. She felt she was yelling her answer. "No, I work."

"You don't talk on the phone?"

Alex shrugged. Her head flopped from side to side. She'd fallen so far inside herself she found speaking nearly impossible. She was beyond drunk. Everything had become hazy and faded in and out. She was talking, but she wasn't sure what the questions or her answers were. She heard the words "Sedona" and "Crystal" but didn't know what he was asking. Or how she was answering.

She was horrified when she heard herself chuckling and saying, "I don't know. Spirits. You're kidnapping them." She didn't know what else she said.

She heard JT laugh but didn't know why.

Everything was so far away and fuzzy. Her voice said, "Tomorrow. Crack of dawn. Best energy." She faded out but came back when she heard her mouth say, "Cathedral Rock."

Sometime later, she found herself in her apartment bathroom, her head over the toilet bowl. It was coming out red and watery. A lot of it.

She crumpled onto the cold marble floor and wiped her mouth with toilet paper. The vomiting got some alcohol out, and she could think a bit more clearly.

"*Fuck!*" she screamed to the walls. She banged her head against the toilet bowl as she sat up. "*Fuck!*"

The exertion made her vomit again. How could so much be in her? As she emptied more of her stomach, the realization hit her. He'd drugged her. On top of the alcohol.

She finished and collapsed back onto the floor. It all made sense. It was all a setup. He'd hired her to find Crystal and probably spy on the

Network. And he wanted to hurt Alex along the way because he was a sick, evil person.

Alex shakily sat up. "I have so fucked everything up," she slurred. "I've killed Crystal." She bent over the bowl and threw up again.

She got on her hands and knees and pulled herself up, then staggered to the kitchen and drank as much water as she could. She searched her space, looking for one of her four cell phones. She had to warn them; JT was probably on his way there.

The phones were nowhere to be found. Maybe, in her blackout, she'd put them in her Birkin. Alex found the bag and rummaged through it. She poured the contents onto the table. Where were they? She couldn't find any of them, not her two Las Vegas cells or her Sedona phone. The burner. Alex stumbled into her bedroom. She'd left it in her nightstand. She pulled open the drawer, but that phone was also missing.

Alex knew she was drunk, but she always had at least one phone on her. She'd taken both her Vegas phones to dinner.

JT. He must have found out about her burner and taken all her phones. Alex let out a loud groan. Her laptop. She should have phone numbers on her laptop. She staggered out to her living room, but her computer wasn't in its usual place on her coffee table. She searched the room but couldn't find it anywhere. JT must have taken all her devices, so she had no way of warning everyone in Sedona.

Helplessly, Alex looked around the room, trying to think through her drug-induced haze.

She had to get to Sedona. As fast as possible. She looked at her watch. It was midnight. It took around five hours to drive there, so if she left immediately, maybe she could warn them at the rock.

Alex phoned the twenty-four-hour concierge, praying JT hadn't told the receptionist to keep Alex there.

"Layla, I need a driver in ten minutes to take me to Sedona. They can use my Audi. Then back when I'm ready."

"Do you know for how long?"

"Probably a day at most." Alex felt her thick tongue slur her words.

"Thank you. Meet the driver in the parking garage. The attendant will take care of you."

"Thanks."

Alex hung up and rushed around her apartment. She fell twice as she changed her clothes.

She buzzed the concierge again. "Can someone put coffee in the car for me?"

"Done."

She hung up, unable to think. She grabbed an overnight bag and stuffed in whatever she thought she might need: toothbrush, deodorant, change of clothes. Alex straightened up. What was she doing? She wasn't going on vacation. She threw the bag on the floor and grabbed several Vitamin Waters and her wallet before staggering to the garage.

***

Hours before dawn, Dr. Max and Zak packed the Range Rover with the scientist's equipment. Hank carried Crystal and put her in the backseat of Dr. Max's Prius. Sharlene and Jackie went with Hank while Zak joined the scientist. Hank pulled out first in the eco-car, with Zak following. To avoid traffic and potentially being seen, they took the longer route, toward Cottonwood and out to Beaverhead Flats Road, so they could come in on the backside of Cathedral Rock.

They parked in the dirt parking lot and headed for the trail, their headlamps lighting the way. Hank carried Crystal as they made their way along

Oak Creek and around brush and tree limbs. Eventually, they connected with the main trail and made their way toward the great rock of Sedona.

Sharlene led the way like a graceful mountain goat, her silver muumuu shining in the moonlight and flowing about her. Her headlamp gave her an angelic glow as she stopped and looked back. Jackie smiled and waved, doing her best to control her huffing and puffing. Hauling lab equipment at 4,500 feet made moving harder than usual. She adjusted her headlamp and continued down the trail.

Sharlene held up her hand. "We can stop here." She pointed to a small, sandy area just off the trail and next to Oak Creek. "The energy's as powerful here as farther up, and it's better to be near water."

"And away from hikers who'll be here soon," said Jackie.

Dr. Max put down the two cases he carried. He bent over, breathing hard. His headlamp tumbled off his head and onto the sand. "I need to work out more," he said, grabbing his light and standing up.

"I'm with you," Jackie said. "Can I help?"

Dr. Max shoved the lamp haphazardly onto the top of his mushroom cloud hair. "Give me a couple of minutes to set up and calibrate my machine."

"Hank, keep an eye out for anyone on the trail," Sharlene said. She started to turn but stopped. "And remember that people hike here. Don't go shooting anyone."

Hank raised an eyebrow and gave her a quick nod.

Sharlene pulled an assortment of stones and some vials of liquid from her backpack. She busied herself placing the rocks around the area and pouring liquid onto the various pieces of quartz and crystals as she softly sang in a language Jackie didn't understand. Possibly Native American or even Tibetan. She wasn't sure.

Dr. Max and Zak opened two of the cases and pulled out the machine they'd all built over the past few days. Dr. Max busied himself with assembling the equipment. The Crystalizer looked somewhat like a mixing board in a recording studio, with dozens of knobs and switches all over the console. From the machine's center rose a metal rod with a crisscross structure built around it. The quantum computer rested below. Zak connected what looked like two car batteries.

Dr. Max turned on the Crystalizer. Lights flashed and blinked across the console. He took readings and calibrated the machine.

Jackie walked over and sat next to Crystal.

Crystal took her hand. "Hi," she whispered, opening one eye.

"Hey, you," Jackie replied. "Don't leave us now. We got here."

Crystal smiled and closed her eyes. Her body began phasing in and out.

"Zak," Jackie said. "I think you and Max need to hurry."

"We're just about there," Zak said.

Dr. Max straightened up, his headlamp falling off again. This time he left it on the ground. "We have it."

"What do we do now?" asked Jackie.

Sharlene walked over to Crystal at the edge of the river. She motioned for the others to create a semicircle around her.

"Step back some more," Dr. Max said from behind the machine.

The group took three large steps back.

"Hank, can you help Crystal sit up?" Sharlene asked.

Hank lifted Crystal and leaned her against a rock before joining the semicircle.

"Everyone, relax," Sharlene instructed. "You don't have to do anything."

Dr. Max nodded to Sharlene, who started chanting again, this time louder.

The scientist turned up the machine. Blue and white lights flashed brighter as a soft hum filled the air.

Jackie felt a light vibration in her body. It started in her heart area and spread throughout her chest. It buzzed through her feet.

Dr. Max walked over and placed a small calibrator near Crystal's head. "Everyone, step back more," he said, looking at the reading. He walked back to the Crystalizer. "The machine's going to build in intensity, and we don't want to get caught in the beam it'll create."

They all stepped farther away from Crystal.

Dr. Max yelled over the noise of the machine. "Hank, can you help Crystal stand?"

Hank walked over to the fallen spirit as she pulled herself up on the rock. He steadied her as she straightened to her full height, then moved a safe distance away.

The Crystalizer buzzed louder and made a crackling noise. The metal rod coming out of the console vibrated and glowed as the entire machine hummed. A beam of bluish white light shot from the rod and enveloped Crystal.

Her body glowed from the inside out, bathed in quantum warmth.

Jackie gasped as light flowed from the crown of Crystal's head and shot up toward the sky, as if the heavens were calling her home.

***

Once they were out of Las Vegas, there was little traffic, aside from eighteen wheelers speeding to their destination. When Alex opened her eyes nearly five hours later, she saw the outline of the red rock formations ahead of her. Drool dribbled from the side of her mouth; Alex wiped it away with her sleeve. JT would have flown, so he could have found them already and killed Crystal or done whatever he planned to do.

She sat up and grabbed the thermos of coffee. She was grateful for the sharpening effect of caffeine as she guzzled a few mouthfuls. Alex had a splitting headache and was sure she was still drunk and drugged.

She assumed Sharlene wouldn't use the main trail to Cathedral Rock. Even before sunrise, there would be tourists. They would stay off the top also for the same reason.

"By the way," Alex said to the driver. "What's your name?"

"Booker, ma'am."

"Thanks for bringing me all this way, Booker."

The driver gave her a warm smile through the rearview mirror and nodded.

Alex directed him down a gravel and dirt road to a parking lot with only two cars. The sky was getting light enough for her to see. She got out and leaned against the limo to regain her balance. The Range Rover in front of her looked like the one from Network headquarters. The other one was a Prius, and Alex knew JT would never be seen in a car like that. It was a good sign.

With no phone or flashlight, Alex looked around in the semidarkness.

Booker leaned out the window. "Want me to come with you, Miss Scott?"

Alex shook her head, swaying slightly. "I'm fine. I'll be at least an hour, possibly longer." She looked around at the outline of desert, rocks, and trees.

"Thank you, Miss Scott. Take your time." He nodded and shut the window.

Alex started to walk away but stopped. She went back to the car and tapped on the glass as she leaned against the door to steady herself.

Booker lowered the window. "Yes, ma'am?"

"Alex, call me Alex."

Booker smiled but said nothing.

Alex pointed off toward the field. "If anyone comes, I went that way. Got it?"

The driver nodded and leaned back in his seat. "Yes, ma'am."

"Thanks. I owe you."

Booker leaned back and slid his hat over his eyes. "You don't owe me anything, Miss Scott. I'll be here." He closed the window.

Alex made her way out of the parking lot and down the dirt road to the river. She would look for Crystal on Templeton trail. Hopefully, if JT showed up, he'd get lost on the one she pointed out to Booker.

***

JT's private plane landed a couple of hours before Alex. He'd rushed to the main Cathedral Rock trailhead, but Shooter, Pop, and Trigger couldn't find anyone except a stray tourist fumbling in the dark to the top of the rock. Hiking in the pitch-black was ridiculous to the global kingpin. In fact, to him, any kind of hiking itself was pointless. He stayed in the car and popped stormtrooper stomach tabs while sipping his processed protein shake. The private contractors milled about outside the car.

Shooter clicked off his tracking device and looked at JT through the SUV's open window. "She just got here and parked. We can find them."

"You'd better. Get me there now." JT held back the urge to strangle the mercenaries from The Society. "I can't believe you incompetents couldn't find them. Good thing she came here."

Pop entered the coordinates into the GPS and sped toward Alex's last-known position in the Oak Creek Village area.

JT let out a long "pfffffffffffffffffttttt." The driver coughed, so he farted again, this time on purpose. It was a smelly one.

Within twenty minutes, they were pulling into the Baldwin Trail parking lot. JT saw the three parked cars and recognized the one he'd gotten for Alex. Good thing he'd put trackers on all the company vehicles.

As soon as the car stopped, Shooter, Trigger, and Pop jumped out and rushed to the Audi's window. JT sauntered over behind them. Trigger banged on the glass.

"Which direction did she go?" JT barked as he approached the car.

Booker rubbed his eyes.

"Do you want your job? Which direction?"

The driver slowly nodded toward the trail Alex had instructed him to point to less than twenty minutes earlier.

JT and the three gunmen ran off toward the back side of Cathedral Rock.

***

Carefully, Alex made her way down the trail, doing her best to avoid the rocks and tree roots. She walked on the path but kept veering to the right and left. Her breath came in quick gasps. The lack of exercise, the alcohol, and whatever drugs JT had given her put her at a snail's pace. She crossed an open space on a wide, sandy trail. She saw tracks in the sand, like something had been dragged recently. A good sign.

Alex stopped to catch her breath. Her heart pounded in her throat. Glancing down the path, she saw movement. A bright light shot up from a clearing ahead of her.

"Crystal!" she cried as she staggered forward. "Jackie!"

Alex stumbled and fell face first in the sand. Footsteps ran toward her.

***

JT followed his security force up the trail. "Ow," he cried as a branch hit him in the face. "Be careful, you idiot," he said to Shooter as the gunman led the way.

"Yes, *sir*," rang out in the semi-dark.

"Not so loud," JT said as he tripped over a tree root. "They'll hear you."

"It's one way or the other," Shooter replied. "A loud 'yes' or a soft one."

"Soft now, you moron," JT said as he kicked a rock. "Fuck. That hurt."

"Gotta watch where you walk," Trigger said as he nimbly followed behind.

JT turned, "Shut your....fuuuuu."

JT fell flat on his face. Trigger and Pop hopped over him.

"Those rocks will get you every time," Pop said as he and Trigger kept walking. JT could hear them both laughing.

"One!" JT barked to his assistant. "Get me up."

One of Five rushed over and pulled JT to a sitting position. "Oh, dear," he said as he rummaged through his bag. He pulled out a white cloth and began dabbing at JT's nose.

"Oww, that fucking hurts," JT screeched.

"I've got to get the blood off."

"Blood? What blood?" JT grabbed the cloth and looked at it. In the growing light he could see that it was stained a dark color.

One pulled out another cloth and finished cleaning up JT, though his nose continued to bleed.

"Just shove the cloth up his nose," Shooter hollered over. "It'll stop the flow."

JT snatched the hand towel from One of Five as his assistant tried to push it up his boss's nose. "Don't fucking do that." He threw the towel to the side. "Just get me up."

One helped JT to his feet. "It might be broken sir."

"I don't fucking care. Just get me to them."

The assistant put his arm around JT and helped him walk down the trail. The three mercenaries stared but said nothing.

The sky brightened with the start of dawn as they continued. JT saw the sheer terracotta cliff of Cathedral Rock towering up to his right. A creek flowed to their left.

Shooter held up his hand and clenched it into a fist. Trigger and Pop stopped silently behind him. JT continued to hobble forward with One at his side, but the head gunman held him back.

"What are you doing?" JT hissed. "They're right there. I hear them." He pointed. "I think that white light is also a giveaway, you idiot."

"Assessing the situation, sir."

"Well, assess my ass."

JT pushed past the security force and made One help him up the trail toward Crystal.

***

Hank leaned over and helped Alex to her feet.

"JT. On his way," she managed to say as she gasped for air.

Hank whistled a loud bird call. Within seconds, Jackie and Zak rushed down the path.

"Oh, no," Jackie said, approaching Alex.

"Still drugged," Alex slurred as she tried to catch her breath. "JT. Coming."

"Let's go back," Jackie said. "Zak, help me take Alex." She turned to Hank. "Follow and cover us."

Hank gave her a sharp nod and pulled out his Glock. He walked backwards as he aimed it at the trail Alex had come from.

The four made their way to the clearing where Dr. Max stood at his machine. Crystal was enveloped in a beam of bluish-white light as she leaned against a boulder at the creek's edge.

Sharlene hurried over. Jackie and Zak lowered Alex onto a large rock by the water. Sharlene sat next to her and shooed away the other two. "Go help Crystal. I'll stay with Alex." She looked at Hank. "You too, Hank. Protect Crystal."

Hank followed Jackie and Zak to the edge of the river near their spirit friend. He kept his gun trained on the trail they'd just come from.

Alex saw the glowing bluish-white light and made out Crystal in the center. They'd started, and she wasn't too late. Perhaps she'd done something right.

Sharlene slumped and slid off the rock, her silver muumuu floating gracefully around her. Alex watched in disbelief as she crumpled silently into the sand.

Alex turned and watched Hank fall silently to the ground. Zak crumpled next to him. She didn't understand; it was a dream. Everything was in slow motion. Jackie collapsed next to Hank.

Alex looked up dazed and saw JT's evil eyes leaning into her face, his nose dripping with blood. He cackled as he brandished some type of weapon. Three military-clad men followed. He held up his hand for them to stop.

JT grabbed Alex and pulled her off the rock before dragging her to the creek's edge. "I can't wait to get you alone," he hissed in her ear. "I'm going to hurt you like you've never been hurt before." Roughly, he gripped her arm until Alex cried out in pain.

Fear ripped through her body. Playtime was over. He wanted her to suffer. Alex froze and flashed back to the abuse and humiliation from her childhood, and to the pain that haunted her no matter where she went. She clearly saw the pattern of abuse that had chased her for her entire life. She was living in hell.

She struggled with something deep inside herself, a power that had kept her paralyzed and cloaked in fear her entire life. It scolded and yelled at her nonstop, criticizing her every move and letting her know she was worthless and didn't deserve happiness.

In a flash, Alex understood. She'd taken over from her parents. They didn't need to criticize and berate her anymore; she'd been doing it to herself her entire adult life. Her mother had planted seeds of shame and self-hatred inside her since she was born. As Alex grew, the bullying and abuse from those around her fertilized and watered her self disgust until she'd created a dark and demeaning part of her psyche that had taken on a life of its own. The soul-destroying entity had kept her from the happiness she deserved and kept her repeating the same patterns of abuse for decades. And that dark force was herself. Alex had been controlled by no one other than herself.

Alex struggled with her monsters. She realized that by turning all the abuse she'd suffered back onto herself, by blaming herself and thinking she'd done something wrong, she was creating what happened to her. She was creating her reality. That dark, ugly energy from her past had taken root inside her and was controlling her life. Alex was abusing herself.

Something inside snapped. Even in her drugged and drunken state, Alex knew she was done. If she allowed JT to hurt her again, he would kill her, or she would do it herself. The humiliation and reality of knowing the dreams she'd had for herself were nothing more than nightmares that she was creating were too much to bear.

Alex exploded. She fought JT with all her might. She bit him as hard as she could and relished his cry. She wriggled out of his grip, but he lunged forward and grabbed her arm. He smacked her in the face. In return, she kicked him between the legs with all her might. He squealed and bent over.

"Pick her up," JT said with seething anger to his lead mercenary. "All the way."

Shooter grabbed Alex and lifted her in the air above him.

Alex left her body and escaped into the back of her head. She could see what was happening, but nothing registered in her body or mind. This was the end. She'd never had a chance at life.

JT straightened and stepped back. "Throw her in. Hard."

In slow motion, Alex flew through the air. She saw the water beneath her, the dawn breaking through the surrounding trees. She wasn't scared; she wasn't worried. She felt a certain relief at knowing it was all over. Alex embraced the inevitable.

As she started to fall, she glanced at Crystal pulsating in the blue white light. They locked eyes.

"I'm sorry," Alex mouthed as she fell into the cold, dark water. Her world went black.

***

Sign up for news about the next book in *The Mind Monsters Series: The Journey Home*
dianehatz.com/sign-up/

Also by Diane Hatz

All versions of **Fallen Spirits** at Books2read.com/Fallen-Spirits

Buy the first book in *The Mind Monsters Series*:
Rock Gods & Messy Monsters – Books2read.com/RGMM

#1 Amazon Hot New Release in:
Absurdist Fiction
Pop Culture
Pop Culture Music

Awards:
Eric Hoffer Award, Science Fiction & Fantasy 2024 (1st Runner Up)
Eric Hoffer Award Grand Prize 2024 (Short List Finalist)
Da Vinci Eye Award 2024 (Finalist)
First Horizon Award 2024 (Finalist)
BookBub New Releases for Less (Sept 2022)
The Wishing Shelf Awards 2023 (Finalist)
Indie BRAG Medallion (Winner)
Foreward INDIES 2023 (Finalist)
The International Review of Books 2023 (Starred Review)
Independent Book Review Top 30 Impressive Books 2022
BookBub Most Frequently Wishlisted Book (Dec 2022)

Stay in Touch

Please help an indie author by leaving a review — it helps more than you know! Thanks!

Sign up for Diane's email list and newsletter!
dianehatz.com/sign-up/

Get exclusives and support my work on Patreon —
patreon.com/DianeHatz
Part of a book club? Visit dianehatz.com for sample discussion questions.

Instagram & Facebook – @dianehatz.author
YouTube – @DianeHatz
Patreon – patreon.com/DianeHatz

Blog – dianehatz.com/blog/
Substack – dianehatz.substack.com/
Medium – dianehatz.medium.com/

Acknowledgements

Many thanks to everyone who's encouraged me on my roller coaster to self fulfillment, including:

HHDL, Zoe H, and all my spiritual guides

Beta readers – Leks Drakos and Jennie Vercouteren

Robin Vuchnich from My Customer Book Cover for the cover design
Heidi Baxter for the headshots and event photos

My writing group in The Writers Room – especially Carrie, Noemie, Jaime, Sadie, Stacy, and Tulani

And to the Universe, for giving me the opportunity to do what I've always wanted—write books!

Thank you all!

About the author

 Diane Hatz is a multi-talented author, organizer, and inner activist. Her debut novel, *Rock Gods & Messy Monsters,* has earned numerous honors, including first runner-up for the 2024 Eric Hoffer Award in Science Fiction & Fantasy and #1 Amazon Hot New Release in three categories. Her second book, *Fallen Spirits*, continues her creative journey.

Diane's writing is humorous, sci-fi-tinged satire and social commentary on themes such as materialism, corporate greed, spirituality, and finding oneself. Though fictional, her writing is based on her experiences, observations, and spiritual path. She has been a follower of The Dalai Lama for over twenty-five years.

Diane received a Master's in Creative Writing in London, England.

After thirty years in NYC, Diane moved to Santa Fe, New Mexico, where she currently lives and writes. When not creating, you can find her wandering the desert, road tripping, and helping abandoned dogs find homes.

Made in the USA
Columbia, SC
15 August 2024

40076502R00140